# FIRE FUN AND FANTASY

Written by Ellen Fleming

Copyright ©

All rights reserved

ELLEN FLEMING (2023)

## Acknowledgements

Thank you, Christine Robertson, for your patience in compiling my book. I could not have done it without you. Tom McKendrick, for the fantastic artistic front cover. Many thanks to the Clydebank Writers Group, for inspiration, especially Jill Smith for her extra help.

(www.clydebankwriters.com)

I wish to thank my husband Jim, our children, grandchildren, and great grandchildren, for listening to my poems, stories, and whatever other scribblings that I had written. I love you all, always.

*"No, not another one?" They would laugh.*

I would like to give a very special thank you to my Granddaughter Elizabeth. Who helped me immensely on the way to finally publish.

## Forward

I joined Clydebank writers 11 years ago. I love writing and listening to others reading what they have written. I studied HND acting and performance as a mature student. I then went on to lecture, being employed by Reid Kerr College in Paisley. I taught students with 'Special Needs,' as an outreach lecturer. It was very fulfilling, challenging work. When I retired, I joined the Clydebank writers, together with 'All Stars', an amateur dramatic group. I feel that those two hobbies go together with each other.

If you would like to read more of my work, please log onto www.clydebankwriters.com

I hope you enjoy reading my poems, short stories, and other musings.

## Table of contents

8. THE NIGHT MY FATHER CRIED

10. WAN SINGER WAN SONG

14. CORONA

15. ASPECTS OF LIFE

17. MY DREAM

19. BEYOND THE POOL

50. YE CANNAE GIE A HUG

52. TEARS AND LAUGHTER - 1

54. TEARS AND LAUGHTER - 2

55. THE OVERTURE

57. THAT FATEFUL DAY

60. NOTHINGS REALLY FREE

63. WILD AND WONDERFUL

64. BEAUTY VERSUS DEATH

65. INTOXICATING ANGEL

66. SUMMER TIME IN SICILY

68. BEDTIME

69. BALLAD OF LOST LOVE

70. A SECRET LOVE

73. BANG BANG

74. YER IN ROMA

76. POP

78. MY OLD AND TRUSTED FRIEND

80. THE GREASY SPOON

82. IT'S A MAN THING

86. THE DANCE FLOOR

88. NO NAME

90. WRITERS BLOCK

91. OH, NOT TO HAVE MUSIC

93. VICTORIA

94. ARE YE DANCING?   - A PLAY

113. AN ODE TO NANCY

116. NANCY'S TALE

118.  MY PHOBIA

121.  CAREFUL PLANNING – A STORY

129.  MY FAVOURITE SONG

131. MA MAMMY

135. IS IT HAUNTED?

138. DAE YE REMEMBER?

141.  THE BLUEBELL WOODS

143. MY FIRST KISS

146. THE PLAN

147. LOVE HURTS

149. YE BANKS AND BRAES O' CLYDEBANK TOON

151. THE KING'S ABDICATION

157. A KNIFE THROUGH MY HEART

159. ALL HALLOW S EVE

161. DIFFERENT WORLDS

164. THE PHONE CALL

166. HEAD TO TOE

168. THE WONDERFUL BAY

171. WORD POWER

173. YE KNOW, YE KNOW

174. I AM NEITHER

176. JACK

178. THE BUTCHRCRATIC OATH

181. THE IRISH BOAT

185. THE BEAUTY I SEE

186. GOD'S GIFT

187. MAGS AND TAM

190. AN UNFORTUNATE AFFAIR

193. JUST WAN MAIR

## THE NIGHT MY FATHER CRIED

My dad was a fireman. I remember vividly him taking me to Ingram Street Fire Station, when I was a child and laughing, when he slid down the pole to show me how quickly he could reach the fire engine.

On 28th March 1960, Dad came home from work, settled, and was looking forward to reading in peace and quiet. But that was not to be! He had laughed and joked with his friends and colleagues, who were starting their night duty.

At 7.49 on that night, 1 million gallons of whisky and 31 thousand gallons of rum in the warehouses at Cheapside Street Glasgow, exploded in a horrific blaze.

We had no telephone phone in those days, so news was slow and long reaching us. A banging on the door that night, warned us that something was badly wrong. Dad's brother Joe came charging in "Is our Hugh on nights?" he asked. My mother said, "He's in his room." Joe's face was filled with dread.

Uncle Jack who lived in the city had telephoned Uncle Joe. He heard a rumbling explosion and went to see them. "I will never forget that hellish sight and the thunder", Jack he reminisced.
"The front of a warehouse came crashing down, they say there's many dead".

Jack said he had heard the fearful screams, then an eerie silence fell. The blaze rose high and lit the sky, just like the fires of hell.

Far away, in Drumchapel our hearts were filled with fear. We saw the blazing sky alight, the inferno felt so near. I remember sitting praying for all the men within our hearts. My father was a brave and courageous man, with no hesitation in fighting. All able hands were called that night, all the men from our tenement block. We lived in a fireman's close, there being only firemen living there.

Nineteen men perished on that night, fourteen firemen and five salvage corps men. My dad didn't arrive home until next day. I'll never forget his haunted eyes ...his face, sooty and dirty, streaked with tears. He had helped to pull his dead friends from the smouldering pyre. Imagine how that must have felt?

Requiem Mass was held in St Andrew's and the funeral service in Glasgow Cathedral in the High Street The streets were thronged with people, who had come to pay their respects. Dad was a pallbearer at St Andrew's Cathedral. The dead were buried in Glasgow Necropolis. A monument stands to this day, their names dedicated to 'Britain's worst peacetime disaster'.
The Fire Service, Police, Ambulance and Lifeboat people devote their lives to saving others' lives. Many have given their own lives in serving. We should never forget when we hear the sirens: brave people are putting their lives on the line for us all, just as my dad did.

## WAN SINGER WAN SONG

It was a Saturday night, my dad had asked a few friends round for drinks, when I say a few friends, I mean four of their favourites. Mary, Wullie, Phil and Aggie. who were my parents Lizzie & Hugh's best friends, dad known as Shuggie.

I can just imagine, dad in the pub. 'Why don't you awe come tae mine fur a wee swally, Saturday eh?' It was the late sixties, I was a teenager, hated those Saturday night soirees. They were awful, mum would put bowls of crisps and nuts on the coffee table; her posh fare was grapefruits with cocktail sticks full of pickled onions, squares of cheese and pineapple chunks; the grapefruits looked like hedgehogs. 'Awe that's lovely,' Mary and Aggie would gush, 'ye shouldnh'ae have gone tae awe that trouble Lizzie.' 'Oh, it's no trouble ladies, only a few wee bits and bobs.' Secretly she enjoyed their praise. She thought she was a cut above Mary and Aggie.

Saturday night came, and it was the usual scenario. Mum in her best dress, she wore a dress with about 5 underskirts which made her dress stick out like a ballerina's. Dad was casual, he hated dressing up. The 2 other couples came in. Aggie was mutton dressed as lamb. She had on a black pencil skirt, white blouse, great big white high heels, and black tights. She looked and walked like a penguin.
Mary was a bit demurer with a twin set and pearls. Food set on the table, oohing and aahing, 'awe ye shouldnh'ae gone to all that trouble,' bla bla bla. I went to my room to listen to top of the pops, but I could hear all the banter.

'Whose fur a swally?' Dad had started pouring the drinks. 'Ach I'll just have a wee sherry,' mum said. I knew a wee sherry was just for show. Mum was an attention seeker; she was waiting to see what the other women asked for. Mary and Aggie both wanted whisky. 'Ehhh I'll just have a whisky too, instead of the sherry. Just a wee wan mind.' Mum could be posh and slang in one sentence. She knew full well that dad would give her the same measure as the rest. Then the party really started. 'Gies a song' Phil said, 'come oan Shuggie, it's your hoose, you have tae start the party.' In those days a sing song was the entertainment.

'Gies Kathleen,' Said Wullie. Kathleen was my dad's favourite song. He didn't have to be asked twice. I knew he was desperate to sing. 'Kathleen so fair and bright ehh', he belted out in a shaky voice. They all sang in shaky voices back then and the end always ended in ehh. At the chorus, everyone joined in.' Order order wan singer wan song Wullie shouted'.

'Right Lizzie, it's your turn.' 'Oh no my voice is not as good as it used to be.' Mary elbowed Aggie and whispered; 'whit makes her think she was any good in the first place.' They both giggled. 'Come oan Lizzie gies a Steak and Kidney number,' meaning a Sydney Devine song. 'No! No someone else go before me.' She obviously wanted to be coaxed. Aggie opened her mouth to sing; 'Aha aha, hold on Aggie I'll gie it a try.' Doing her posh and slang thing again. 'O the crystal chandelier lights up the painting on the wall.' Mum sang out. Again, at the chorus they all joined in. Wullie shouted 'order order, wan singer wan song.' Scottish, Irish, Sydney Devine's Crystal Chandelier and Tinyeee bub-bells, (tiny bubbles) to Dean Martin's Little Ol' Wine drinker me, were all murdered.

'Jean?' My dad was shouting at me. 'What?' 'Bring us yer gramophone.' 'Oh, dad it's not called a gramophone now, It's a record player.' 'Whitever the hell it's called, bring it here, we're sung oot.' I brought my record player down to the living room. There were no cd players back then, it was all vinyl.

Dad had a few records, the Clancy Brothers, the Corries and wait for it! The Celtic song. I was praying he would not play that one. How wrong I was? Seconds later Glen Daly was belting out. So, it's a grand auld team to play for.

Awe! 'Wait a minute!' Wullie shouted, 'haud oan, haud oan, enough, enough there's nae need fur that.' 'It's ma hoose and I can play whit I like.' 'Oh, is that right, oot the back and we'll see aboot that,' Wullie retorted. They both staggered out to the back court.

'Come oan ya, ya wee Proddie. I'll show ye aye I'll show ye.' 'Awe will ye noo? A will ya wee eh eh pape.' 'Hello hello we are the Billy Boys; we are the PEO-PELL' (people). Wullie bellowed. Their sleeves were rolled up and their fists were clenched. 'Stop It', Mary shouted; 'yer dancing around there like a pair o' eejits,' Lizzie was crying, saying, 'the polis 'll come and ye'll baith get arrested.' No posh voice! Phil was trying to get into the middle of them. The neighbours were all looking out of their windows enjoying the spectacle. I heard one woman say, 'this is a rare Saturday nights entertainment. Better than the telly.'

Not a punch was thrown, they danced around each other, faces like beetroots clenching their puny little fists, baring their teeth, and repeating, 'I'll get ye,' 'Naw ye'll no,' 'I'll get you.' No if I get you first.' Just as Wullie was about to land Shuggie a punch on the face, a screeching, howling, wail came in unison, they sounded like two banshees bellowing in the country. 'AHHHHH whit the f….' They were drenched, looked like drowned rats. Aggie had thrown a bucket of water over them from the upstairs window. She couldn't have aimed any better; drowning them in midstream.

Mary and my mum shouted up. 'Well done Aggie that'll teach that pair o' numpties.' Phil the peacemaker, said 'come oan boys let's get you inside, dried and have a wee cup o' tea tae heat yis up.'

Phil put the kettle on while mum found some dry clothes. They both came into the living room looking very subdued. I think the bucket of water had sobered them up. 'Right shake hands,' Mary commanded.

They looked at each other for a minute, then shook hands. 'Awe a didn'ae mean whit a said Shuggie.' 'Naw neither did I Wullie.' They patted each other on the back. Phil came in with the tea.

'That'll no heat us up Phil,??? Whit we need is another haulf.' 'Aye' Wullie beamed, 'let's get this party back oan track.' My mum in her posh accent reiterated. 'No more party songs Hugh.' 'Agreed?' 'Aye agreed Lizzie.' But Wullie's voice was heard above all. 'Jist remember!' Wan singer wan song.'

## CORONA

It started in China this hateful Corona

Now it's dancing around in Verona

Parliament is in suspension.

Oh! My God will it affect my pension?

Toilet roll fights and hand gel scraps

What will we use when doing craps

We'll go to jail with these awful crimes.

So just wipe your bum

With the financial times.

Corona corona just change our luck

Please do the right thing

And just get tae fuck.

## ASPECTS OF LIFE

Birds with their wings sailing in the sunlight,
The lazy cat sleeping by the door.
Allowing the birds their freedom 'for now,'
Roof tops glistening with snow,

Smoke billowing from the chimney pots,
Cows chewing the cud from hay.
That the farmer had brought from the silo,
A meandering river, gurgling, enjoying its sleepy way to the sea.

Milk maids in clogs, setting about their daily toil,
Ample wife indoors, cooking delights for the day,
Buttermilk scones, treats she knew was the way to her husband's heart.
Dogs playing in the yard.
Barking and growling at unwanted strangers.

Trees their arms waving in the gentle breeze.
Creating a noise that was both musical and calming.
Farmers toiling the soil and eating from its gifts.
Enjoying the food of life.
A world without malice, how wonderful?

Ragamuffins rummaging in polluted middens,
Beggars, street urchins and pickpockets,
Servants, whom the rich treated
Like the growling and barking dogs in the farmyard.

A ring of roses they sang,
Cholera, dysentery, diphtheria.
Dying children clinging to their mother's empty breast

For succour they could not claim.

No phones or mobiles to spoil their peace,
No computers or social networks to invade their privacy,
No cars to pollute their precious air,
No planes, no continental treats,
NO N.H.S.

## MY DREAM

I've always wanted to write a book,
So, to a writer's class myself I took.
They threw me in right at the start,
Showed me a house, then said,
Write about that.

I was confused and, in a muddle,
My pen was poised, oh what a fuddle,
About a house, what can I write?
I was ready to take flight.

They read out loud,
I could not compete,
I was shaking from head to feet.

Pen to paper I did put,
Then they said
Now read it oot.

I felt faint and said oh no,
I think it's time for me to go.
They locked the doors and kept me in,
I didn't want to make a din.

I read it out to my distress,
Oh dear! It's not quite for the press.
I came out and gave a sigh,
To the writer's class I waved bye bye.

Then I thought, it might not be bad,
Another try? I may be glad,
So next week came and I walked steady.

With pen and paper to the ready.

They were all waiting, I said, oh no!
Again, I thought it's time to go.
We then were told to write a story,
I decided mine would be gory.
I wrote about a gang that berated,
And about how I was treated,
The class then said let's look,
Perhaps one day I'll write that book?

## BEYOND THE POOL

I watched his chest rise and fall. He was so handsome, his long dark eyelashes a striking contrast to his beautiful light blue eyes. Long eyelashes more befitting to a woman were flickering in repose. The bile rose in my throat, I hated loathed and despised this beautiful monster who lay before me. This creature that I had once loved.

I met him at work. He was an architect, owned the company, I was his P.A. I first walked into his office when I secured the job of my dreams. He was so tall, his hair was dark, rather shaggy which enhanced his appearance. In contrast I was small, petite, long blond hair brown eyes with lashes that could not compete. Pretty, not beautiful like Simon. I loved working there. I never thought I had a chance with my employer, but a girl could dream. He was going out with a beautiful girl who worked in the office. I would only see her fleetingly as we worked in different departments.

I had a good job in Glasgow as a P.A in an architect's company. I loved my Job and was good at it. I was engaged to Mark, one of the architects in the company. We had planned our wedding.

Everything seemed perfect, then I found out Mark had been cheating on me with another girl in the office. The old cliché everyone knew but me. I had to get away. I was so humiliated.

My mum said, 'Lisa you don't have to run away, there's plenty more where he came from.' 'Mum it's time for me to have a fresh start. I've sent my C.V to various companies in London and I think I've found my perfect job. The same as I was doing here but the pay is fabulous, and I've found a wee flat just round the corner. It has two bedrooms so you can come and visit any time. It's only five hours on the train, or an hour to fly.' Mum hugged me and gave me her blessing.

I arrived in Euston, my little flat was in Bayswater only a tube ride away. The company I was going to work for was walking distance from the tube station; S R Architects. Simon Ritchie, who owned the company, would be my boss. I felt so privileged to be the owner's PA. I was to start on Monday. My flat was beautifully furnished. I had the weekend to explore my new surroundings. Decided I loved London.

I arrived at work a little early. Wanted to make sure I could find my bearings. It was a tall, elegant building with a plush interior. Simon's office was on the top floor with views over Hyde Park. The whole top of the building had floor to ceiling windows and the skyline was magnificent. I tapped the door lightly at 9pm prompt. A beautiful, elegant girl swept past me. She turned. 'Are you Simon's new P.A?'

'Yes,' I stammered. She laughed. 'Just go in, would you like a coffee? Simon's never here till 9.30. You'll get to know the routine soon.' 'I'm Jenny.' I shook her hand and said, 'I'm Lisa lovely to meet you.' Our friendship was sealed.

Jenny was beautiful inside and out. We had another friend, Anne. The three of us would meet for lunch. Jenny and Anne took me round all the London sights exploring. We went to the Tower of London, Buckingham Palace, and the London Eye. At night we went clubbing. I was a young independent woman working in London in a fabulous job, great friends, and a great night life. My mum came to visit often. Life was good.

Simon was lovely to work for. Sometimes I found it hard to keep my eyes off him. One day when I was deep in thought about some building project, we were working on. A voice said 'Lisa.' I jumped; it sounded like a command. I looked up and Simon stood laughing. 'I didn't mean to startle you,' he smiled. 'I wondered if you would like to join me for lunch.' That was the beginning of our relationship.

He was wonderful, treated me like a princess. Flowers, chocolates, jewellery. I started losing touch with Jenny and Anne. I didn't really notice as I was so in love with him. Jenny would ask me out for lunch or a girlie night. When I said I would go and told Simon, he would arrange something else for that night. I would put my girlfriends off. One day Jenny asked. What is it with you Lisa?' 'We don't see you anymore. I know you're going out with Simon, but surely you could make some time for us?'

One day when I did get the chance to meet Jenny for lunch I asked. 'Did you know Simon's ex-girlfriend?' He never speaks of her and when I ask, he gets angry and tells me it's none of my business.' Jenny said 'rumour has it that they had a big bust up and she left him. He probably doesn't like talking about it. I think she dumped him?'

'Mm I told him about my relationship with Mark and how I was cheated on.' You'd think he would open up to me about his ex.' Jenny nodded. 'You know 'what men are like, pride and all that shit.' 'What was her name?' I questioned. 'She left not long after I started, didn't she? 'I only saw her occasionally,'

Jenny frowned. 'I think her name was Sandra Dixon. She was a lovely girl, I knew her when she first started, and we used to go for lunch together. But just like you all that stopped when she went out with Simon. She lived with him. He has a big house out in Buckinghamshire somewhere. Apparently, it's fabulous. Anyway, once she left nobody saw her again, she was quiet and kept to herself. I thought strange, I'd never been to his house?

Life went on. I was besotted with Simon. He was a bit of a loner, didn't have many male friends apart from his colleagues at work. He was always charming to everyone. I loved being his girlfriend, really didn't care if I didn't see much of Anne or Jenny. Anne then announced she was getting married and was pregnant with twin boys. Left the company and we lost touch. Until much later.

One night Simon and I were in bed together when I broached the subject of never being asked to his house. He gave me a cuddle and said, 'It's much easier here Lisa, commuting can be a pain and I love your little flat, it's so cosy. I will take you there someday, I promise.' I was going to say, but your other girlfriend lived there with you, but thought no! I won't spoil the moment. So, life went on as usual.

We had been going out together for 6 months, when Simon said. 'Lisa I've booked a little table at Clos Maggiore for tonight. A car will pick you up at seven'. Clos Maggiore was our favourite restaurant. Very expensive. It was in Covent Garden. French/Tuscan. I was ready on the dot of seven. I wore a clingy red dress, matching accessories. Simon always liked things to match. I looked in the mirror and thought, I looked? How do I describe how I looked? In one word. Hot.

Simon was there when I arrived. He had booked a table underneath flowers and branches, a weave of intricate tapestry. I always thought when we went there that I was transported to a little Tuscan village. He gave a soft whistle when he saw me. He laughed and said 'will we just skip dinner and go home right now for dessert.' 'That would be lovely.' I retorted, 'but I'm bloody starving.'

Simon ordered as he always did. I never thought anything of it. As a wee Lassie from Glasgow, I didn't question his gastronomic superiority. I always enjoyed his choice.

Our meal was delicious, the wine was superb according to Simon. I wouldn't know. I excused myself to go to the toilet. When I returned there was a bottle of Dom Pérignon chilling in an ice bucket. 'Oh! What's the occasion?' I laughed as I sat down. 'Lisa, I don't want any fuss, do you understand?' I looked at him in confusion. He then put the little box in front and commanded that I open it. Inside was a beautiful diamond solitaire. He didn't say a word, just slipped it onto my finger and then said. 'Well?' I was ready to squeal yes, yes when he put his hand up to stop me. 'Just nod.' I did as I was asked but I was bursting inside. I felt like jumping on the table and squealing.

Simon went home that night. I was a little upset; after all, we had just got engaged. I couldn't persuade him to come home with me. 'We'll celebrate later.' He said. 'I have another surprise for you.' And at that he kissed me in the limousine at my front door.

I phoned my mum first thing in the morning. She was happy but not as happy as I had expected. I knew she wasn't that keen on Simon, would say things like 'where are your friends Lisa? You always had loads of friends in Glasgow. Sometimes I think Simon's too sweet to be wholesome?' 'Mum' I would bellow. 'Simon is always lovely to you; he treats you great.' 'Ach hen, am yer mammy and want ye tae be happy but I'm jist a wee Glesga wuman, whit dae a know?'

I then phoned Jenny. She was over the moon when I asked if she would be my bridesmaid. 'When's the wedding?' She bubbled. 'Are you having a hen night. When are we going shopping for your dress, and mine? Is it going to be a big wedding, are you inviting your friends from Glasgow?'

By the time I got off the phone I was exhausted. I laughed at her exuberance, and how pleased she was for me. I was still at such a high after last night. I never really thought about what it entailed, and how long the engagement would last.

\*\*\*

I was busy with an important project when Simon approached. He said, 'Lisa, pack a bag we're going away for the weekend. Leaving after work on Friday.' 'Where are we going'? I said, showing my excitement. 'I told you I had another surprise for you, so just make sure you're ready on Friday.' He commanded. 'Yes Sir' and saluted him in jest. He smiled and walked away. He could be gruff at times but that was just his way.

I wondered where he was taking me. It was a beautiful day. We were in his silver open top Mercedes. The wind was in my face. It was exhilarating. I was so excited. We left the Smoke, and soon were driving through beautiful green rolling countryside. A tree lined driveway opened out to reveal a large Mock Tudor Mansion. I thought, wow! Luxury hotel.

The front garden was manicured within an inch of its life. Part was sunken with a beautiful fountain in the centre. I was so mesmerised that I didn't notice Simon extracting the keys from his pocket. 'Welcome to your new home, ' he laughed. He carried me over the threshold. 'Oi' I joked 'we're not married yet.' 'No' he said, 'but in three weeks you will be Mrs Simon Ritchie. We will be married here.'

I gasped at the interior. It too was Mock Tudor. I almost expected Henry the V111 to greet us. It had a warmth and a modern twist. The lounge was furnished exquisitely. There was a massive open fireplace and a beautiful picture window looking on to the front gardens and fountain. I imagined myself sitting here in the winter beside a roaring fire.

The dining room was furnished fit for a banquet. All the 10 bedrooms had four poster beds and ensuites. Then the kitchen. I couldn't believe it. Wooden beams on a low ceiling. An Aga cooker, a huge table that looked as though it had been cut straight from an oak tree. And chairs with heart shapes cut in their backs.

He then steered me out to the south facing garden. I gasped. Right in the middle was the most beautiful swimming pool I had ever seen. It was surrounded by luxury sun loungers. There was a hot tub and a little wooden hut that housed a shower, piles of fluffy towels and dressing gowns.

'This will be your home in three weeks Lisa. Beautiful, even if I say it myself, perfect peace with no neighbours for miles around. Do you know I designed this house myself?' He boasted. I looked over at the view. It was breath-taking. He put his arms around my shoulders. 'That's the Chilterns in the distance.'

I hated my Glaswegian ignorance. What is the Chiltern?' He laughed. 'The Chilterns are a range of hills of great beauty. You will be able to feast your eyes on them every day when we're married.'

I started to plan what I would wear; what Jenny would wear. I phoned my mum and asked her to come down. She was so excited to be the mother of the bride. I was her only child; my dad had died three years ago. There was only me and mum. "We only have three weeks mum; I'll book you a flight right away. I can't wait for you to see Simon's house.

\*\*\*

Simon came into the office one day. I was engrossed in what I was doing. 'Lisa' he said, can I have a word? We are having a small intimate wedding. As you know 'I'm not one for fuss.' I looked at him confused. He had a massive house, why wouldn't he want a lavish wedding to show it off. 'You can still have your mum and Jenny.' He said sternly, but that's it. Kevin from I.T will be my best man, I'll invite some more colleagues from work, there will be about thirty max. Oh and there will be no hen night, understand? I hate women going out dressed as tarts to celebrate getting married.' At that he walked out and banked the door shut.

I was shocked. I thought he'd fallen out with me the way he spoke. I had been looking forward to inviting some of my friends from Glasgow. Having a hooley before the wedding. However, I knew he was a very private person so I just accepted that was how it would be. I was just glad that my mum and Jenny would be there. I didn't know many from the office as I worked exclusively for Simon.

He then dropped another bombshell. 'Lisa, I want to come with you to choose your dress, Jenny's and you mum's outfits.' 'What?' I gasped. Don't you know its unlucky for you to see the bride's dress before the wedding?' 'Stupid superstition' he scowled.

'Simon, I do not want you to see my dress. I want it to be a surprise for you.' There was no reasoning, so I just gave in like I always did. Not so my wee Glesga mammy. 'Nae man is gonnie tell me whit tae wear at ma only daughter's wedding, so ye kin tell Simon tae get stuffed. I just laughed knowing my mum would get her own way.

When I told Jenny she was shocked. 'What no hen do?' 'Simon doesn't approve of women making fools of themselves?' She looked at me and said, 'Lisa, is this your wedding or just Simons?' 'Och, you know what he's like Jenny, he's a very private person, doesn't like a fuss.' Jenny intoned. 'Sounds to me as though he's a wee bit controlling Lisa?' 'Oh! Jenny how can you say that? Simon's the kindest person I know.' 'Ok Lisa if you say so.' She gave me a hug. 'We'll have a wee champagne lunch when yer wee mammy comes doon,' she said in her best Glasgow accent. We both laughed.

Simon chose a very simple dress for me in champagne. It was nice, classy. I might have even chosen it myself. Jenny was in an apple green dress. Again, very simple and stylish, I wasn't keen on the colour. I'd heard that green was unlucky for a wedding. Mum was lovely in a powder blue dress, matching jacket, and hat. She looked very elegant.

The wedding was everything I expected, not like the lavish one that Mark, and I had chosen. I could see Simon was right. A very stylish but quiet affair hosting around thirty guests.

The dining room was stuffed with food and drink buffet style. No top table or speeches, although Simon did thank everyone for coming and toasted. 'To my beautiful wife.' He kissed me. It was so touching I felt tears in my eyes.

We danced round the fairy lit pool. Most of the guests stayed overnight including my mum, Jenny and her boyfriend Paul. I had forgotten to tell Simon that Paul had been invited. He took me aside and said 'Lisa, never again invite someone to my home without my approval.'

I was upset and said, 'I didn't think you'd mind? Paul is lovely and he's Jenny's boyfriend.' He looked at me strangely. 'Have you met this Paul before?' I stammered, 'well, yes Jenny and I had coffee one afternoon, she invited Paul along. I forgot to tell you about the wedding plans and everything.' His eyes were cold, and he whispered, 'Lisa you must always tell me who you meet, stranger or no stranger; do you understand.' Tears began to well in my eyes. My wedding was beginning to turn sour. He smiled and took me in his arms. I forgave him instantly.

Everyone was leaving the next day. I tried to persuade my mum to stay a little bit longer, but she insisted. 'Naw hen it's your honeymoon, ye widnae want yer wee mammy playin' gooseberry noo wid ye?'

I laughed at her broad Glasgow accent. Simon hated it. If I ever lapsed, he would say 'Lisa, I don't mind your lilt, but I hate your broad accent'. He gave my mum a kiss and said 'bye Mary' then went in and shut the door. He had ordered a limousine to take her to the airport.

I walked out with her. She gave me a hug, kissed me and said, 'I love you Lisa, be careful.' 'Mum look at these surroundings. What do I have to be careful of.' She looked at me sadly, gave me a hug and was gone.

I never saw her again. She died of lung cancer three months later. Simon and I went to her funeral. I was heartbroken. I was all alone now apart from Simon. I made a mental note to get in touch with Jenny.

\*\*\*

Simon didn't want a honeymoon abroad. 'Look at your surroundings Lisa, why go abroad when we have this.' He was right, we had total solitude, made love by the pool. Laughed and frolicked in the water, made love again.

Life was good. One night I cooked a beautiful dinner. His favourite, leg of lamb with all the trimmings. I had set the table with candles glowing setting the atmosphere. He sat down, his face sombre. 'The honeymoon is over now Lisa. I'm back to work tomorrow. But you can take it off.'

I didn't think anything of it. Thought he was being nice. I cleared the dishes away and prepared to go to bed. As I was doing the dishes a thought occurred. Not once did Simon offer to clear up or cook a meal. The flowers, chocolates and jewellery presents had also stopped.

Simon had a cleaning lady. I thought he had given her time off so we could have some privacy during our honeymoon period. I became skivvy at that time. I didn't mind but thought it odd. After all, it was our honeymoon.

Maybe he really did want complete privacy. We never went over the door the whole time and I didn't complain.

I climbed into bed. 'What kept you?' It sounded like a snarl. 'Sorry Simon I tidied up; I know you don't like to get up to a mess in the morning.' He put his arms around me, and we made love. It seemed different this time, almost aggressive, rough not tender like before. Afterwards he leaned up on one elbow, peered into my face and said 'You do know you belong to me Lisa.' Not I love you, Lisa? A strange cold feeling crept over me. I fell into a restless sleep. Something had changed and I couldn't figure out what?

He got up for work in the morning. I said 'thanks for letting me have a bit more time off work Simon. It's really appreciated. 'I'll take the rest of the week, but I'll come in on Monday. Looking forward to getting back, although it was great spending our time here after the wedding.

He looked at me strangely. 'You won't be coming back Lisa.' 'What'? I stammered. 'I want you here to be a proper wife to me.' 'But I will be a proper wife to you Simon. Lots of married women work. Any friends I've ever had have worked when they married. 'Well not mine' he bellowed. 'But we have your cleaning lady here in the mornings.' 'Not anymore,' he sneered. 'I've sacked her because she was surplus to requirements.' At that he swept out and banged the door shut.

I felt claustrophobic if that was possible in such a large house. What was happening to me? I sat down and wondered what would I do? We had not been over the door since our wedding. Was I to be kept prisoner? I thought maybe a compromise. I lifted the phone and dialled Simon at work.

'Hi Simon, I was just thinking what if I came in part time. I understand that seeing each other 24/7 is maybe not a good idea, but I could get a transfer to another department, and I'd still be home in the afternoon to clean and cook dinner.'

'It is not up for discussion Lisa, and while we are on the phone, I must tell you to never call me at work again, do you understand?' I went to speak but the line went dead. What was happening to me? A few months ago, I was a happy go lucky woman with a job, a lovely man, or so I thought. Here I was now a prisoner in my own home.

Life meandered on. He watched my every move. I was only allowed to go to the shops and back. He even checked the mileage in my car. I had no friends. I'd lost touch with Jenny and Anne. There was nowhere really to go. 'Why do you want to go out anyway Lisa, you have everything here?'

One day I was in the supermarket when I saw Anne with her twin boy's. I couldn't believe it. 'Hi Lisa.' she enthused. 'What are you doing here Anne; I thought you still lived in London?' 'We moved not long after the boys were born, we live in High Wycombe now, much nicer than London for the children.' 'Oh!' I said, 'that's only about an hour away from us.'

'Lisa, I phoned the office to ask Simon your phone number and address, but he was always busy.' 'Yes, he's a busy man' I smiled. I knew he wouldn't speak to Anne. He was slowly isolating me.

'Look, why don't you come, say Thursday. The boys will love it, they can play by the pool.' 'You have a pool?' 'Yes', I laughed. I wouldn't dare ask her round at the weekend when Simon was here, but what he didn't see would do him no harm.

Anne arrived with her twins. I had prepared lunch, pizza, chicken nuggets, juice for the boys and nice wine for Anne and myself. The boys squealed and splashed in the pool. It was a lovely sultry summer day. Anne and I sipped our wine. We had two glasses each. I was going to open another bottle, but Anne said 'I would love to Lisa, maybe another time when I don't have the boys' 'Of course' I said. 'How silly and irresponsible of me. Don't think when you've no children.'

'Don't worry I'm sure you'll produce a brood.' She laughed. 'None on the horizon,' I smiled. 'Lisa, I hear you're not working now?' 'No Anne, Simon likes me at home.' She frowned. 'And what do you like Lisa?' 'Oh, I stuttered. I love being here, just look at the place I want for nothing.'

We had such a lovely day. I cleared all the remnants of Anne being here and opened another bottle of wine.

It was such a lovely evening I lost track of time and fell asleep on the sun lounger. I was woken by a roar. 'WHAT THE FUCK DO YOU THINK YOU'RE DOING?' I jumped. 'Where is my fucking dinner?'

He grabbed me by the hair and threw me into the pool. I struggled up choking and spluttering while he was standing naked. 'Get out' he commanded. I tried to pull myself out. He yanked me by the hand's hair and arms, tore off my swimming costume and raped me on the lounger.

This was to become a regular occurrence. He took my phone away, started doing the shopping himself and locked the front door. I could only go out to the pool which had a ten-foot wall. He had it built not long after we married. 'Security.' He said. I could only see the tip of the Chilterns beyond the pool. I had no money; he even confiscated my car. I was a prisoner in my own home. Or should I say Simons. Home.

A while after the Anne incident I had been thinking how lovely it was to have children's laughter in the house. We hadn't had pool games for a while, and I wondered if I should broach the subject? I decided to make us a nice dinner. His favourite leg of lamb, a nice bottle of wine. Create a relaxed mood. I set the table at the pool. It was a beautiful starlit evening, candles flickering in the moonlight. Lovely setting to ask the question that was on my mind.

'This looks lovely Lisa what's the occasion?' 'Just thought it was such a nice evening we'd have dinner by the pool.' He came over and kissed me. 'Splendid idea. Funny I was thinking the same', he sat down, and I brought out the lamb with the trimmings. He sliced the lamb and put the vegetables onto his plate. I hesitated. 'Erm Simon I was thinking,' he continued eating, not looking up. So, I stopped. 'You were thinking what?' 'Well since I'm not working now, I was thinking that maybe we could have a baby?'

His face darkened. He lifted his plate of food and fired it into the pool. It scattered over the patio, sun loungers and floated on the water. He screamed, 'there will be no children ever, do you understand.'

He then lifted me, and I followed the food into the water. He jumped in after me held me under till I thought I was going to drown, he then dragged me out and raped me as before. When he had finished, he screamed. 'Clear this mess up bitch and never mention children again.'

\*\*\*

This physical and mental abuse continued. He called it our pool games. Each time he did I thought, 'is this the day that I'm going to die?' I started drinking. I would drink in the morning when he left for work in the early afternoons then go to bed, sleep, and sober up for him coming home at night. I had to have his dinner on the table by six, or else I'd be treated to a pool game.

I couldn't believe I was allowing this to happen. I'd read about women who suffered abuse, much less than me and wondered how they could allow it. And here I was doing exactly the same.

I thought about escaping. But where would I go? He had taken my liberty. He had locked up my clothes. All I had was a pair of jogging bottoms, an old jumper, a tee shirt, and a jacket for shopping, which I didn't do any more. I had no money, no car, nothing.

Simon had Valium in the bathroom cabinet. I started taking them. But was frightened that with the drink I wouldn't cope so I just stuck to vodka. I was told it wouldn't smell of alcohol on your breath. I was so good at keeping it a secret and he never noticed.

On rare occasions we went out for dinner. He would choose what I would wear. He always wanted me to look nice. When we got home, he would look me up and down. 'You looked like a whore tonight I saw men ogling you. You were loving it.'

Then we would have pool games. I couldn't argue that it was him that had chosen the clothes for me. He was a sick perverted bastard. I knew I had to get away from him otherwise he would kill me.

One day he came home from work and said Kevin had invited us to dinner on Saturday. I was so excited. I was getting out of this mansion prison. 'Get smartened up for Saturday, you look like something out of Belsen' he snarled. I hadn't really been eating, just picking at my food and the drink wasn't helping my looks.

Saturday arrived, I hadn't had a drink all week and tried to eat more than was normal for me. He chose a green velvet dress with matching accessories. He liked everything matching. I thought I looked nice with my slim figure. He looked me up and down and said, 'You'll do but you're too skinny and your face is gaunt.'

We arrived at Kevin's on the dot of seven. Simon was always punctual to the second. Kevin had a beautiful house, not as grand as ours but there was a lovely, homely feeling. His wife June greeted us. You could tell how in love they were. They were so free with each other. Simon never left my side. He was frightened I would stray and tell someone the truth. When we were in the taxi, he instructed me what to say, how happy we were and what a wonderful husband he was.

The doorbell rang and I jumped. Our doorbell never rang. Kevin was greeting someone at the door, and there stood Jenny and Paul. I went to go over to greet them, but Simon held me back. Eventually she saw me. Squealed and rushed over. She threw her arms round me and hugged me tight. 'Lisa, I've missed you so much, how are you?'

'I heard you weren't well, Simon said you were very poorly when I asked you both to our wedding. You're so thin.' I got a warning look from Simon. 'Yes, I was very ill Jenny, couldn't even have visitors.' 'Did you get the flowers?' Jenny said, 'I gave them to Simon?' 'Oh yes I got them Jenny.' I never received any flowers. 'Thank you, sorry I didn't phone, but I was so weak.' She gave me a hug and said, 'don't worry I understand.' 'Glad you and Paul tied the knot.' I said.

After dinner I excused myself to go to the toilet. I fully expected Simon to be waiting outside but Jenny was there instead. She hustled me back into the toilet. 'Lisa, what's going on? You look dreadful. I don't believe all that cock and bull story about you not being well. But by the look of you you're not far off it. What is happening to you?' I wanted to cry but couldn't for fear Simon would notice. I whispered. 'Come on Wednesday.'

I tried to make the best of myself on Wednesday. Simon had all my nice clothes locked away. I only had my jogging bottoms and tee shirt.

I always had a swimming costume or bikini to hand as he liked pulling them off me for our pool games. That was almost the only time we would have sex.

I put on my swimming costume with a pair of jogging bottoms. It was a nice day. I looked a bit presentable. I took a bottle of vodka out of Simon's extensive wine cellar. I had stopped drinking wine. I couldn't replace it. Simon was a wine snob and didn't touch spirits. So, when a bottle of vodka was finished, I would replace it with water and put it discreetly back in its place. He would kill me if he found out.

Jenny rang the bell at 9.30. I already had vodka, as was my usual start to the day. I had to sleep. I usually went to bed around one so I could shower and be sober for Simon coming home at six. He never really noticed me now anyway. He would eat, and if there were no 'pool games,' he would go into his study, and I wouldn't see him again till we went to bed. He always insisted we slept together. We sometimes had bed games, where he would handcuff me.

I had managed to get a hold of a spare key. Simon always locked me in. The pool area was the only place that I could go outside as it was surrounded by a ten-foot wall as I said earlier. I opened the door and let Jenny in. I hugged her and asked if she would like a vodka and we could sit at the pool. She looked at me strangely and said sternly.

'Lisa no I do not want a vodka at 9.30 in the morning. What are you doing to yourself?' She lifted the bottle and poured the vodka down the sink. I didn't care there was plenty more where that came from?

'What is going on?' Jenny asked. I just looked at her and burst into tears. I cried and sobbed till I thought I would die. Jenny put her arms round me and said. 'Get it all out Lisa, I'm here for you.' I then poured my heart out. Told her everything. All about the pool games and his cruelty. 'Lisa go and pack a case and come with me?' 'Pack a case?' I laughed. 'I have no clothes Jenny. He has them all locked up. I often wonder what happened to his ex, Sandra Dixon. He has a room that is locked, that is where he keeps all my clothes, jewellery etc.' Jenny looked thoughtful and said. 'I've often thought of that myself. No one has seen her since she went to live with Simon. I've heard she has no family. Her parents were killed in a car crash.'

'I can't come with you Jenny.' 'I have no clothes, no money, nothing.' Jenny looked thoughtful. 'Look, I'll tell you what. Give me those spare keys in case he realises you have them. I'll come tomorrow with some clothes for you, let myself in, do not, and I mean do not drink vodka.'

When Jenny left, I felt uplifted. For the first time my spirits rose. But that was not the only spirits that rose. I went to the cellar and got myself another bottle of vodka.

I sat at the pool, drank the whole bottle, and fell fast asleep. The next thing I knew I had landed on the patio with Simon standing over me. He had upended the lounger. He screamed. You fucking alcoholic cunt. Get up. I hadn't heard the c word since I'd left Glasgow. I scrambled to my feet; I thought this is it I'm going to die. I was shivering, with fear and cold. He stormed into the house and came back out with handcuffs. Put your hands together. I defied him and said no as I backed away. His face got red; he walked back into the house. I thought, am I going to get away with it? No chance, he came storming out with ankle manacles I had never seen before. This was it. I was going to die.

He was so tall he overpowered me. He punched me in the face, I reeled back and fell. He stood over me laughing. He then ripped the clothes off me and raped me, and said 'I can't really make love to you with your ankles cuffed now, can I?'

He handcuffed me, then put the ankle cuffs on me. I thought if he throws me in the pool, I'm dead. He then lifted me and that is exactly what he did. I sank, struggled but there was nothing I could do. I could feel my lungs filling with water and I started losing consciousness.

The next thing I woke up by the pool. My hands and feet were free. He snarled. 'Not quite yet my lovely, now go and make my fucking dinner.'

I noticed then that he was drunk, there was a bottle of vodka sitting next to him. It was strange he never drank vodka. Thank God he'd picked vodka instead of water or

I really would have died. I thought I really do have to get away.

\*\*\*

As I started preparing Simon's dinner a thought occurred to me. He was really drunk with the vodka. I had never seen him drunk before. He always liked to be in control. I went into the kitchen where we usually ate. I stammered. 'Simon, do you want wine with your dinner?' 'Of course, I want fucking wine wench. Ha ha skinny fucking wench with no tits.' He slapped me on the bottom and bellowed 'and no arse. A wench without tits and arse. At least my new wench has tits and an arse.' I was dumbfounded. So, he was having an affair. Poor bitch God help her if she was to replace me.

This made my plan even more viable. He liked his red wine to breathe. I crept up to our ensuite where he kept the Valium prescribed to him. He never took it. I always wondered why he had it. Funny he never hid it from me? I emptied the bottle. Wondered how many it would take to knock him out till morning.

There were about ten in the bottle. I didn't want to kill him just yet. I thought five; with the amount of vodka and wine he had consumed I figured it would knock him out till morning. And if it killed him? Well Ce la vie.

I crushed five tablets; I was going to put them into his wine, but decided to put them into his spaghetti

Bolognese. I thought the crushed tablets might fall to the bottom of his wine glass and he wouldn't drink it all,

or maybe he would notice. Not a chance I was prepared to take. I watched him gobble down his dinner drink all the wine and a good skinful of vodka. Now I would just need to wait and see what would happen?

He staggered out to the pool and fell fast asleep. I went up to the medicine box again. I knew what I wanted. I cut four pieces of Tubi grip. Didn't want marks on his wrists and ankles. I then went down to the pool, carefully slipped them on to his wrists and ankles. He was out for the count. I Did the same with the handcuffs and ankle manacles that had a small chain between them.

All I had to do now was to wait till morning. I had left him sleeping by the pool. I threw a blanket over him and went to bed. It was the best sleep I'd had since I married him a year ago.

I got up in the morning and went down to the pool. I stood and watched his chest rise and fall. He was so handsome his long dark eyelashes, a striking contrast to his beautiful light blue eyes, more befitting to a woman, were flickering in repose. I hated, loathed and despised this beautiful monster, whom I'd once loved.

The door opened right on 9.30. Jenny shouted 'Lisa where are you?' 'I'm at the pool,' I shouted back. She came through, her eyes widened. She looked at Simon sound asleep on the lounger with his hands and feet in cuffs.

'What the hell are you doing Lisa?' 'I'm going to kill him; will you help me?' She backed away. 'Have you lost your mind? I thought we were going to the police today?' 'I've changed my mind. Who would believe me?' She looked at me closely, 'you have a black eye, did he hit you last night'? 'Yes', I said 'and that's not all he did.'

I told her what had happened the night before. She was horrified. 'I have a plan, Jenny. I promise if it goes wrong, I will not implicate you, I just need a little help.' 'Good God Lisa what is your plan?' After careful consideration she agreed to help me. 'Did you bring decent clothes for me to wear?' She pulled out nice jeans and a top. Something to wear for a casual lunch. Perfect.

I pushed him hard and using a word that I had never in my life used I shouted. 'Get up cunt.' He spluttered. 'What? Where am I?' His eyes were bleary with the drink and Valium. I could see he was disorientated. Then he tried to move and discovered he was manacled, wrists and ankles.

He struggled like a madman. 'Not so brave now you fucking psychopath.' I could see the word psychopath really got to him. 'Heard that word before, did Sandra call you that? Where is that poor girl anyway, did you drown her? Just like I'm going to drown you.'

Jenny was in the background; he didn't see her. 'Get up.' I commanded. 'Jenny, I need your help.' He was screaming.' I got a pair of scissors and cut his clothes off. He stood naked. He struggled like hell, but we managed to get him to the edge of the pool. He was still groggy which helped.

He was now so scared he peed himself. 'Oh, how humiliating, I scoffed, and in front of Jenny. Let's clean you up.' We managed to shuffle him to the edge of the pool. I said, 'Pool games on my terms.' He fell just at the edge of the pool where I wanted him to. Blood stained the tiles. He opened his eyes and pleaded. 'Please Lisa?' 'Not this time sunshine' I then rolled him into the pool.

Jenny and I jumped in after him and pulled him to the surface. The water had revived him somewhat. His eyes looked terrified 'You love pool games don't you Simon.' We let him go, watched him struggle till he sank, and waited till we were sure he was gone. Jenny was an excellent swimmer. She jumped in and released him of his manacles and Tubi grip and assured me he was dead.

I made sure no fingerprints were on the handcuffs and manacles then locked them in Sandra's room. We had his clothes that I had cut off him and Tubi grip, hid them in Jenny's car, till it was time to dispose of them.

We drove to High Wycombe where we had arranged to meet Anne in a café, had coffee and cake. It was a lovely early afternoon; we said our goodbyes to Anne and set off with a promise to meet soon.

We drove to a wood near where Anne lived. We set Simon's clothes on fire, waited till they were ashes, then scattered them all over burying them under leaves. We went out to the pool, and there he was floating on the top face down. It wasn't nice, but it was either him or me.

Jenny phoned the police on her mobile. She told them I was too upset to speak. The police and ambulance came to remove the body. The detective said 'It looks like he banged his head at the edge of the pool. Or maybe someone hit him?' He looked at me. Jenny said, 'we were meeting our friend Anne in High Wycombe when we left him on the lounger.'

Can this friend verify this? 'Yes, here's her phone number.' Jenny gave the police her phone number and Anne told them that we'd met her. She was shocked to hear of Simon's demise and told them that there were plenty more people in the café that could give us an alibi.

We may need you down at the station at some point Mrs Ritchie.' 'That's fine detective' I said, as I blew my nose and wiped my crocodile tears. 'Oh and by the way did your husband always swim naked? 'Yes, we hardly ever wore clothes in the summer. We always sat by the pool naked.' 'And your friend didn't mind seeing your husband naked?' Jenny laughed. 'It's nothing I've not seen before. 'We're all very open.' She smiled.

## EPILOGUE

There was an extensive search in the fields beyond the pool looking for a murder weapon. But all they found was poor Sandra Dixon's body. The coroner said it looked like she had died of drowning, but they weren't sure because her body had deteriorated so badly. I could have told them otherwise.

Simon Ritchie obviously couldn't be charged with her murder, but DNA proved it was him. All her clothes were found in the locked room. I had stolen the key from Simon whilst he was asleep, moved my clothes into our bedroom and locked the door where Sandra's clothes were. It was assumed that he had committed suicide with remorse. The Postmortem had revealed there were copious amounts of alcohol and some Valium in his system but not enough to kill him. Or had it been an accident and he had bumped his head on the edge of the pool.

It was declared an open verdict. No murder weapon. I was Simon's sole beneficiary, sold his Mock Tudor Mansion for five million, said goodbye to Jenny, Paul and Anne. Poor Paul was totally unaware of what had gone on between me and Jenny the day Simon died.

I moved back to Scotland. Bought a beautiful house on the banks of Loch Lomond. Now instead of looking beyond the pool to the Chiltern Hills I now look over the loch to see Majestic Ben Lomond. Jenny and Paul visited often, loved it so much they relocated to Glasgow, bought a house on the Lochside not far from me. I got in touch with some of my old friends in Glasgow too. Life was good again.

## YE CANNAE GIE A HUG

You may agree or disagree

Do you remember

When the world was free?

Where people could embrace

And give a kiss upon a face?

A wolf whistle.

Was meant to flatter?

Could be fun with lots of chatter.

We used to be man and woman,

Now our Identity is,

Well! We're just human.

Gentleman's relish is no more,

Just hot sauce, What a bore.

Burger Monarch, they did say.

Think to McDonald's you may stray.

Babies now, not girl nor boy,

Allowed to choose whichever toy.

Will it be birth lines in their folder?

Or will they decide when they're older?

Am I right or am I wrong?

In this new age

Do I belong?

## TEARS AND LAUGHTER – 1

My mother cried yer Granda's deid

Fell doon the stairs and banged his heid.

We were shocked and cried a river.

Thought Granddad would last forever.

He had lived a hundred years.

Got his kicks from wine and beers.

That turned up carpet in the hall.

Was the cause of Granda's fall.

The funeral was a great success

We laughed and cried and made a mess.

Wee Shuggie wanted tae start a fight

It was Granddad's Day, it wisn'ae right.

Ma mammie shouted; don't you dare.

And promptly grabbed him by the hair.

Granddad would have loved his wake

My mum had baked a great big cake.

We even sang his favourite song.

Laughed out loud at times now gone.

We had a hooley, it was a ball.

All because of Granddad's fall.

## TEARS AND LAUGHTER - 2

Tears and laughter emotions of joy and sadness

You can feel happy and cry.

And sad as you laugh.

Granda's funeral was just that, we cried at the church.

And laughed at the wake.

Films, dramas, and books have the same effect.

To cry is good lets out the grief

To laugh it's said helps you live longer.

I'd rather laugh than cry.

But the two emotions

Go side by side.

I've laughed till I cried.

And cried till I've laughed.

Tears running down my eyes.

Not knowing if I'm sad or happy.

But crying does not always turn into laughter.

And laughter does not always turn to tears.

The same but oh so different in our hour of need.

## THE OVERTURE

Stalagmites and stalactites

It begged beyond belief,

We walked down into the cave.

To see what was beneath.


Porto Cristo was the place.

Way out in sunny Spain,

The beautiful Majorcan Isle

Where it doesn't often rain.


When we reached the caves cold depths

There was a lovely lake,

The lights went out, we gasped!

Must be a mistake?


Then came a twinkle.

The water rippled,

No one was quite sure?

When a boat came sailing,

Orchestra on board,

Playing an overture.


When ascending to the top

I hope you will agree.

The Caves of Drach, lake and overture

Was a magic sight to see.

## THAT FATEFUL DAY

The house, full of wonderful aromas, our beautiful home,

Pancakes, waffles eggs from our chickens

Sweet succulent honey from our bees,

Life was good.

Father, reading his paper,

Mother cooking breakfast,

Me upstairs, 12 years old packing school bags, ready for the day.

Dad a doctor, well respected.

'Outside. Outside!' They shouted.

Front door banging wood against wood.

Frightening sounds.

They came in that fateful day,

Gun barrels wrecking our beautiful home.

Smashed eggs, plates, crockery,

Creating a mosaic floor.

'Outside, outside,' they roared again.

Pushing, shoving, humiliating.

Crowds of neighbours cowering in the frozen weather.

Some in nightgowns and pyjamas.

Frail old people cold and shivering.

"My wife," he pleaded, "please my wife?"

"Come here," they commanded.

"My wife, she is old and frail,"

"She needs clothes; a blanket?" He beseeched.

"Bring her here, you'll both soon be warm".

Walking hand in hand they obeyed.

Standing together 160 years between them

Rifles cocked; loud shots echoed

Blood, prostrate figures, the ground had met them.

Poor old couple, gone forever.


The crowd gasped and reeled.

"Any more requests?"  They sneered.

Their upper arms decked with black.

"Your carriage awaits," they shouted.

Handing us shirts with yellow stars.

You have the message now?

My father? I never saw again.

My Mother. She took a shower.

Me. I'll never forget those terrifying messages.

**(Holocaust messages)**

## NOTHINGS REALLY FREE

I was shopping for my tea

When I saw something that was free

I bent down I was quite blind.

When another hand with mine entwined.

She screamed and shouted; I saw it first.

I thought her face was going to burst.


I decided to let go but something in me said oh no

I was annoyed.

Our hands they twisted and they toyed

We grabbed and pulled it was a scene

Her narrow eyes were very mean.


The customers gathered all around

They egged us on it was profound.

The Manager came we were on the floor.

He was going to throw us out the door.

We were fighting at a fast pace.

When a box of eggs fell on her face

The whole shop was in an uproar.

It only was a tiny store.She was swearing and spluttering.

The police were called in

It really was such a terrible din.

There were smiles on their faces

As they sorted it out

It was only over a packet of trout.

Then they looked stern my face it grew pale

I thought they were going to throw us in jail.

I pleaded my case the nerves made me cough.

He said to me madam you sound like a toff.

She laughed then she bellowed her face in a scoff.

Then she screamed

It was my bloody BOGOF.

The policeman he misunderstood.

He thought that she was being rude

But the manager stepped in to let the police see

It means buy one get one free.

The policeman said you both can go

But don't come back I mean it so

We went with nothing for our tea.

And got no buy one get one free

Going out the door was a disgrace.

I got nothing but she had egg on her face.

So, the message is, if you've got to fight for your teaJust remember nothing's free.

## WILD AND WONDERFUL

Crashing; corrupting land

White foaming froth

Grey blue background

Angry yet calm, wild and wonderful.

Housing a world

Beneath an undulating surface.

Beautiful colourful creatures.

Ships ploughing through its immense glory.

For pleasure or trade.

Enter at peril.

## BEAUTY VERSUS DEATH

The tree stood erect.

100 years at least

Reaching to a cloudless sky

Branches swaying, tall, wide, strong.

Birds nesting.

Its foliage restricting view and sun

Leaves causing havoc.

Treacherous to the home environment.

Beauty versus death.

What choice?

## INTOXICATING ANGEL

As life ebbed, he emerged from nowhere.
Head to toe in black shimmering ebony
Magnificent, Majestic, Masculine.
In contrast; a face as white as ivory
Handsome? No! Beautiful!

He beckoned, I followed
Hypnotised by his quintessential beauty.
He floated into a dark deep void.
Equine in his movements.

On he went this alluring, mysterious, mystical creature.
Not a sound nor bird song
No footprints or crack of wood branch
Deafening silence.

Seduced by an intoxicating Angel
Into the bleak, black, bowels of despair.
Nightmare of nightmares,
Transgressions punished for eternity.

## SUMMER TIME IN SICILY

We went to Taormina

Etna stood majestic

Smoke belching from the crater

It really was fantastic.

Sitting on our balcony

We read into the night.

It was so beautiful sitting there.

But the bloody mossies' they did bite.

The next day we had big red welts.

We scratched until they bled.

On that night we read our books

Safely in our bed.

We watched the football in our hotel.

When Ireland won, we cheered.

Jim had a pint to celebrate.

At 8 euros it was in his words

'The drink is effin' dear.'

Sicily was so lovely.

The prices we forgive.

But if one day we do go back

It will be all inclusive

## BEDTIME

He pestered me every night

I couldn't get to sleep.

It got so bad I have to add.

I started counting sheep.

I dreaded when bedtime came.

He would start again.

What could I do to make him stop?

It was driving me insane.

One night when he was at it.

I thought; then I arose.

I gathered up some cotton wool.

And stuffed it up his nose.

I can read your dirty minds.

Now sweep them with a broom

The moral is when your partner snores.

Just use the other room.

## BALLAD OF LOST LOVE

### (To the tune of The House of The Rising Sun)

He laid his head upon her breast.
A shiver touched his soul.
He knew for sure that she was dead.
His heart as black as coal.

They were wed for just one year.
She was his blushing bride.
They laughed and danced and drank their fill.
He'd love her till he died.

He found them in between the sheets.
Arms around each other
He stabbed them both then realised.
He'd killed his wife and brother.

He kissed her lips so pale so cold.
His fingers held her hand.
He raised it up to touch his face.
Eyes on her golden band.

He stabbed them both then realised.
He'd killed his wife and brother.
    X 2

# A SECRET LOVE

It was a beautiful dusky evening; I was waiting in anticipation. We met about four months ago; I had fallen in love the first time I set eyes on him. He had lovely blond hair and beautiful brown eyes; eyes that would melt your heart. His name was Sam. He was coming tonight.

I can't ever remember my husband looking at me the way Sam did. We instantly connected. I knew Sam felt the same.

Time was marching on, the moon began to shine, I couldn't wait. The first time we met, I held him in my arms and kissed his face, he returned the favour. He was so warm it felt so right.

My husband had no idea, oblivious. Sam and I had then met several times and it was always the same. We kissed and held each other so close. I would also have to break the news to my son Colin who was nearly twelve. It would be a shock.

'Sam we'll be together very soon.' I reassured him. He would just look at me with those beautiful eyes, I could see he wasn't sure I was speaking the truth.


The last time we met he was crying when I left. 'I promise we'll be together soon, just be patient my darling, you know I love you very much.' I waved him goodbye and shut the gate gently behind me.

I sat in the chair and switched on the light, anxious for us to be together at last. Poured myself a glass of wine and walked up and down. What was keeping him? My husband and son would be home shortly, then it would be time to tell them. I wanted you Sam here by my side when we broke the news.

I heard a car door shut and ran to the window. It was you! I made you go into the bedroom, 'we'll give them the news together. Don't make a sound. I'll break it to them gently.' He understood the urgency.

Then I heard another car door bang shut, I intended to put on a brave face. 'Hello darling, how was your day' I preened. 'It was awful. I had a terrible day, a day from hell.' He looked at me anxiously. 'Why are you drinking?' He questioned, 'you never drink before I'm home. What's wrong? Have you got something to tell me, you don't look yourself.'

'Look Phil there's something you should know.' 'Oh, what the hell, you're leaving me? You're bloody leaving.' Before I could answer a noise came from the bedroom. This would be the moment; 'what the hell's that noise who have you got hiding in there.'

'Don't go in there not yet' I yelled. I wanted Colin, my son, to witness, it was only fair.'

I heard the front door open and shut, it was Colin home from school, he would be shocked I knew, but it would sort itself out in the end.

Phil was ready to open the bedroom door, find my secret lover. 'No' I shouted again. 'Wait.' I cautiously opened the door. Sam walked out a little gingerly at first, his eyes fixed on Phil. Then he spotted me and ran straight into my arms.

Phil and Colin had always wanted a dog, but I was against it thinking of walking it, the muddy mess, until I visited the dog rescue. Why? I don't really know, something beckoned me, and I fell in love at first sight with Sam the beautiful Cocker Spaniel. Phil and Colin squealed with delight, their eyes lighting up. 'Oh my God.' Phil said, 'I honestly thought you were leaving me; you've been acting so strange these last few months.'

'Yes, I had to keep it a secret for four months. The dog rescue place is very strict. We could have had him a few weeks ago, but I paid to board him till your birthdays.' My husband and son shared a birthday. 'I must admit you both had a rival. I fell in love the minute I laid eyes on him, and I think the feeling was mutual.' 'Oh, so he's your dog' Phil laughed and gave me a hug. Colin joined in. 'Happy birthday dad. Happy birthday Colin. 'I'm afraid we'll just have to share him.' Sam was squeezing in between us and giving us all big wet kisses. But I realised he was trying to get to me. He really was my secret love.

# BANG BANG

### (To the tune of Bang Bang by Cher)

He was dark and I was fair.

I knew my man had an affair.

Bang bang, he took an oath.

Bang bang, I cursed them both.

Bang bang they are dead

Bang bang I shot them in the head.

To the gallows I must go

Thinking when I'm in death row.

Just two shots and then they fell.

Bang bang I'll meet them both in hell.

Now I know I have no hope.

I'll soon be hanging from a rope.

When in court the judge did figure

It was me that pulled the trigger.

Bang bang they both fell

Bang bang I'll be with them in hell.

## YER IN ROMA

**(Sung to the tune 'That's Amore)**

When the moon hits the sky like a big pizza pie

Yer in Roma

When ye sit at the Trevi

Only watter

Nae bevy

In a Roma

Francis comes tae the windae

In the Vatican City

In Roma

He gies ye his blessin'

And reads ye the lesson.

In a Roma

Ye'll get pissed on the vino

Speakin' tally to Tino

He'll no know.

He'll say ciao I go homa.

Ma heeds in a coma

In Roma

The pickpockets look funny.

But they'll steal awe yer money.

In Roma

Where the Lions ate the Christians

In the folly that's the Coli

In Roma


Ye'll sail doon the Tiber.

A sipping a cider

In Roma

When ye see signorina's

Yer no gonnie meet as

Yer too auld

Ye can duck and can dive.

But yer now sixty-five

And in Roma

## POP

You were Husband, Dad, Granda and Pop

We always thought you never would stop.

Alex dear, Betty would say.

A nice cup o' tea on a wee tray.


You would go up with her wee special treat.

Where Mushka and Mittens were at her head and her feet

And just in case you're not sure about that.

They were the beloved dug and the cat.


You wanted to spoil her you loved her so much.

That was your way, and you sure had the touch.

You were kind and gentle all through your life.

Especially to Betty who was your dear wife.

You would say to your children if they were late out.

I'll give you a whisker, meaning a clout.

You were soft with the grandchildren when they did play.

You would ruffle their hair and shout whey hay.

Your family and friends loved you so much.

Children grandchildren great and great great

Five generations in your years eighty-eight

From the eldest down to the tiniest tot

And each of their birthdays you never forgot.

Now you have gone to God up above.

To be with your Betty your only true love.

## MY OLD AND TRUSTED FRIEND

My poor heart is full of woe.

You see it's time for you to go

Battered and worn.

you have seen your day of travels ventures

Work and play

Round the world in days of glory

Your old frame could tell a story.

War and peace you have seen

Reigns of monarchs Kings and Queens

Surrounded by stickers worn and curling

Long lost memories now unfurling.

Places we'd been both near and afar

Some driven to in our old motor car

Your lid is cracked faded and pale.

Just like me old and frail


Your handle I held with much delight.

the hinges now rusted and oh so tight.

Earth sea and sky has been our life.

I never got round to taking a wife.

Wanting to travel I had to be free.

To raise a family was not for me

The nursing home for me does loom.

But they told me for you they had no room.

So now I'm going to take some paint.

Capture you though your old and faint.

Then I'm going to watch you burn

Your ashes I'll put in an urn.

I'll see you always till I'm gone.

Then I'll join you in that urn

Our last journey will be heavens staircase.

Just me and you, my trusted suitcase.

## THE GREASY SPOON

Daddy, are we there yet?
Won't be long now pet.
Daddy I'm hungry, I need to eat soon.
Not long now dear till the next greasy spoon.
I'm starving when will we eat.
Just up ahead and we'll take a seat.
Daddy, I see it, it doesn't look nice.
Don't worry darling it's like sugar and spice.
Daddy that lady she's just going to sneeze.
Her apron's filthy and all covered in grease.
Daddy, I don't think that we should stay.
Let's just get up, we can still run away.
What would you like dearies she said
I don't want to eat here I'd rather be dead.
Daddy, I think I'm going to be sick
Get something down you that'll do the trick.
Napkins from kitchen roll were placed on the table.
Daddy I can't, I don't think I'm able.
I've been here before they serve a good meal.
It's cheap and it's cheerful and they do a good deal.

She brought us big plates full of bacon and eggs.
Black pudding and sausage that looked like fat legs.
She wiped our cutlery on her apron top.
And said enjoy, it won't be a flop.
I looked down at the plateful it was rather nice.
But then I looked round and saw some playful mice

Daddy, I screamed as I jumped on the chair.
Daddy, we need to get right out of here.
She came up to us smiling and looked full of cheer.
As she handed my daddy a glass of cold beer.
Daddy drank his beer real fast.
Where's the toilet he did ask.
It's over there beside that stool.
As she handed him some kitchen roll.
Daddy and I went to go out the door.
Sliding on grease that was there on the floor.
The lady said mind you don't slip.
But you know you can't leave till you give me a tip.
Daddy said here you are Mabel.
As he reached for the handle
that sat on the table.
Outside was fresh and very slick
As I stood on the kerb and made myself sick.
To greasy spoons for me I'll say no
All grown up now I know where to go.
No more sliding on grease, till I do the splits.
It'll be the Hilton, the Savoy or even the Ritz.

## IT'S A MAN THING

We were just about to leave the house for a long weekend in the Lake District. I was really looking forward to the break. Cases were packed ready to go into the car, when, Gary, my husband said, 'have you seen the car keys'? I sighed; it was the usual scenario. Don't get me wrong, I was as guilty as the next for misplacing my purse and keys. To be fair, Gary didn't often lose things, but he could never see anything he was looking for, even if it stared him in the face.

The car keys were there, where he had always put them, but unfortunately, I had hung mine on top of his. I said, 'things don't just jump out at you, sometimes you have to move objects to find what you're looking for.' Keys were found and we were on our way.

We had a lovely weekend, the weather was nice, and the hotel was nice. Overall, I felt refreshed. We were travelling back on the Monday when Gary asked, 'where's the satnav?' I was dozing, 'it's in the glove compartment' I said in a sleepy voice. Rousing myself from my slumber, I looked in the glove compartment, it wasn't there. 'I think you'll need to pull over, it must be on your side.' Gary pulled into a lay-by and was frantically searching in his small glove compartment. 'It's definitely not there!' He looked at me accusingly. 'You must have forgotten to take it.' 'Me?' I shouted; 'we never took it out of the car in the first place, why would we?' 'Move and let me have a look.' I lifted all the junk in the glove compartment and there it was, lodged between his logbook and the instruction book for the car. I stared at him triumphantly and said, 'there it is, you just don't look properly.' He glowered back at me and said 'you must have put it there'. I sighed 'I give up.' The rest of our journey went smoothly.

At home we settled back into our routine. Gary was in the kitchen. 'Would you like a cup of tea?' he shouted. 'That would be lovely,' 'would you like a biscuit?' 'Yes ok'! 'Where are they?' he called back.' They're in the biscuit tin in the cupboard.' 'What cupboard?' 'The one they're always in, next to the fridge.' 'I can't see them.' Frustrated, I went into the kitchen. 'I'd have been quicker making the tea myself', I grumbled, pushing him out of the way. 'There they are behind the coffee tin; don't you ever move objects to see if what you want may be hiding behind something else.' The tea gesture was spoiled, so I ended up making it myself.

The next day Gary had an important meeting at work. 'Have you seen my blue tie; you know the one that goes with this shirt?' 'Gary, it's in the drawer next to your other ties.' 'It's not there'. 'OH MY GOD, you are a nightmare. I'm telling you I put it there myself, get out of my bloody way,' I seethed; I mean I had to get out of bed for this one as he was leaving at 7am. I was not at all pleased; needless to say, I found his tie, but my long lie was ruined.

May I say it's not only, 'do you see my tie' etc. It's the shoe issue. No! Not Louboutin or Jimmy Choo's. It's the 'where's my bloody shoes?' Did you move my shoes last night'? 'I know I took them off where I was sitting.' I was fuming, 'Yes of course I saw your shoes, do you not remember me clomping around in them last night when I was making your dinner?' 'I much prefer your size eights to my size 3 slippers, they're much more comfortable,' I said sarcastically.  He had taken his shoes off in the bedroom. They were neatly put there by himself.

'How did your meeting go?' I asked when he came home that night. 'You look rather bedraggled.' 'Yea,' he stumbled, 'eh it wensh really well.' He sounded a trifle sozzled, and something in his voice made me a little suspicious; I trusted Gary completely, but just that little falter in his voice gave me a funny feeling. 'Ach I might as well tell you Catherine; I knew when he called me Catherine, that something was not quite right. He always called me Cath. I was at a boy's jolly; I went with Stevie and Gerry; I know you're not keen on them, so I didn't let on.' I was really angry, I knew Gerry and Stevie both had an eye for the women, I wouldn't have been pleased, but I wouldn't have stopped him from going. To be fair he didn't go out much. My face fell a little and I sulked, 'You know I wouldn't have stopped you, but you should have told me.' I Made him stew for the next few days.

The weekend came. I was all dressed and ready to go out. I liked to go to town on a Saturday. 'Eh!' Cath did you see money lying on the table next to the phone.' 'No! What money?' 'Eh I gave Gerry a loan of 150 pounds the other night when we went on that ehh boy's jolly.' You gave Gerry a loan of a hundred and fifty pounds?'

'Yes, I knew he was good to give it back, which he did, and I think I left it on the table.' 'Well, I didn't see it.' I'm off into town and I'm not helping you look for it, it'll turn up. 'See you later.' 'Awe Cath help me look,' he whined pathetically I don't have any more money on me, I wanted to go for a pint, and have you seen my glasses?' 'Yes, they are on your head you dumpling.' 'Good luck finding your money,' I shouted as I banged the door shut. 'Have fun searching.' 'Boy's jolly indeed,' I laughed to my friend Sandra as we walked into the Ivy restaurant for afternoon tea. Girl's jolly, Gary's treat.

## THE DANCE FLOOR

**(To the tune of 'Tell Me Ma')**

I was at my brother's wedding.

The venue in a country setting.

We danced and drank and had a fling.

Granddad he got up to sing.

All the guests they mixed so well.

Next day they'll be tales to tell.

A lovely couple the bride and groom

I watched them waltzing round the room.

So, in love, it was so twee

Perhaps someday that would be me?

I was watching in a trance.

When a handsome man asked me to dance.

Then he whizzed me round the floor

I hoped to dance with him some more

Beguiled by his enchanting charm

I fell down and broke my arm.

Sprawled on the floor oh what a sight

I really got a terrible fright.

The man he helped me to my feet

It certainly was not discreet.

I awoke I thought, *awe naw!*

The handsome man had shot the craw.

He had fled into the pale.

And I *was* the next day's fairy tale.


I never saw the man again.

I think he thought I was insane.

The moral is don't go for charm.

 You could fall down and break your arm.

## NO NAME

How unfortunate to have no name

It really is an awful shame.

The teacher nods

Or points a finger

Oh, how often I do linger.

Not waiting for fortune nor fame

I just want her to say my name.

I really was baptised you know.

The holy water it did flow

It ran right down my neck I'm told.

And so, this story does unfold.

I went to school the next day.

Waiting for her; my name to say

I put my head down in my book.

So, to the front I could not look.

I glimpsed her jumping up and down.

And on her brow an awful frown

Her whole face was full of malice.

When she burst forth and shouted

Who the fuck is Alice?

## WRITERS BLOCK

Can't think of anything to write

Please can you help me in my plight

My poor wee brain is in a fog

So, no writing I can log.

I have no inspiration now.

It will come back of that I vow.

I do so like my writing group.

But at the moment

my mind is soup.

So, this is all I have today.

There is no more that I can say.

I hope my fog will disappear.

And I'll be writing within the year.

## OH, NOT TO HAVE MUSIC

### (To the tune of 'Seven Spanish angels)

Oh, not to have music.

And the good ol' rock n roll

Johnny Cash and Willie Nelson

Who Gave us Country and Soul?

Pavarotti and the Tenors

Singing arias galore

Standing ovations

Shouting encore.

Remember the Beatles

The Stones and Dylan

Had their styles.

The Scottish Proclaimers

Who sang 500 Miles.

Oh, not to have music

Jazz and the Blues

If we didn't have the music

Think we'd all be on the booze.

Lordy thank you for the music

The country and soul

Not forgetting

Elvis Presley and the good ol' Rock n Roll.

Yes, the good ol' Rock n Roll

## VICTORIA

### (To the tune of 'Three nights and a Sunday double time' by Matt McGinn)

Victoria what more can I say,

Well, she's the gal who works down in the Bay.

She's got charm and she's got flair

Thinks Jim Fleming's a millionaire.

That's oor gal who works down in the Bay.

Victoria, she drives us all insane

Especially her boss who's, Iain McLean.

Well, she is funny, and she can brag

Thinks Jane Eyre is a rare wee shag,

That's oor gal who works down in the Bay.

You'll always see her smiling never crying

And she takes the piss right oot o' John Mulrine.

Well, she is pretty with long dark hair

And we'd awe miss her if she wisn'ae there,

That's oor gal who works down in the Bay

## ARE YE DANCING?  - A PLAY

Glasgow dance hall. Characters. Mary, Wullie, Mary's mum Maggie and dad Jimmy. Wullie's parents Betty and Alex.

| | |
|---|---|
| Wullie; | Are ye dancin' |
| Mary; | Are ye askin' |
| Wullie; | Aye am askn' |
| Mary; | Awe right am dancin' |
| Wullie; | Whit's yer name |
| Mary; | Mary, what's yours? |
| Wullie | I'm William but everybody calls me Wullie. You can call me Wullie. |
| Mary | Oh, I think I prefer William |
| Wullie | Ok William it is, but only for you. |
| Wullie | Mary yer hair smells lovely. I'm glad it's a Moonie we're dancin' tae. |
| Mary | Oh yer a sweet talker Wull er I mean William (she giggles). Och I'm just going to call you Wullie. It's easier |
| Wullie | (Pulling here closer). Oh, yer lovely Mary |

| | |
|---|---|
| | can a walk you hame? |
| Mary; | I don't know Wullie. If my dad sees us, I'll get a terrible row. |
| Wullie | Whit age are ye Mary? |
| Mary | I'm only sixteen. |
| Wullie | (Laughs and sings) only sixteen only sixteen and I love her so. |
| Mary | Shut up you. |
| Wullie | Well it wis a cue for a song. You know it? |
| Mary | Course I do. |
| Wullie | That'll be oor song. |
| Mary | I've only just danced with you. I don't even know you. |
| Wullie | Believe me Mary that'll be oor song. |

**(In the close three weeks later)**

| | |
|---|---|
| Mary | No Wullie I've told you before. Stop trying it on. |
| Wullie | Awe how no Mary, I've known you fur three weeks noo. |

| | |
|---|---|
| Mary | No Wullie I'm a Catholic, and there is definitely no sex before marriage. |
| Wullie | No even a wee fumble Mary? |
| Mary; | No definitely not. You wouldn't respect me, and anyway you've not even met my Mum and dad! And I've only known you for three weeks. What kind of girl do you think I am? |
| Wullie | And when am I going to meet them? |
| Mary | I don't know? Maybe when we've been seeing each other a wee bit longer. And when you stop your fumbling |
| Wullie | Awe Mary I love ye. |
| Mary | I think I love you too Wullie, but it's too soon. My dad's very strict. He doesn't even know we're seeing each other. |
| Wullie | Whit aboot yer Ma? |
| Mary | I tell my mum everything, but I told her not to breathe a word to my dad. I know |

|   |   |
|---|---|
| | she wouldn't because she's scared of him. |
| | He's never hit her mind. Although, |
| | Sometimes I don't think he's far away. |
| Wullie | That's terrible Mary, but if we become serious; then I'll need tae meet him at some point. |
| Mary | We'll see how it goes Wullie |

**Three months later in Mary's House; Wullie dressed in his best suit, shirt and tie.**

|   |   |
|---|---|
| Wullie | Hello Mr O'Hagan, very pleased to meet you. |
| Jimmy | Humph, Yea' hello, so your Wullie, I take it you were Baptized William, yes? |
| Wullie | Eh! Yes, that's right Mr O'Hagan. William. |
| Jimmy | How old are you, William? |
| Wullie | I'm Seventeen Mr O'Hagan. |
| Jimmy | Tell me William, Mary never said, what's your surname, and what school did you attend? |
| Wullie | My second name is McMillan and I went |

|   |   |
|---|---|
| | to Hamilton Cres. School in Partick. |
| Jimmy | (Face red with anger). You know our Mary's a Catholic. How dare you darken my door, GET OUT GET OUT GET OUT. You're a Protestant. Our Mary can never go with you. GET OUT BEFORE I TAKE YOU BY THE ARSE OF YOUR TROUSERS AND THROUGH YOU OUT. Never see our Mary again. GET ME. (He shouted right up to Wullie's face) |
| Wullie | I'm going, you arrogant bigoted old swine. But I'll tell you this. I will be seeing Mary again because I love her and she loves me, and I would've been willing to have married her in the Chapel. (Wullie walked out slamming the door behind him.) |
| Jimmy | You will never see him again, do you hear me? You hear me our Mary you've never to see him again! |
| Mary | But I love Wullie. He was going to ask your permission to marry me. He's really nice and he would've married me in St. Peters. |
| Jimmy | O V E R …M Y …D E A D …B O D Y …Once |

|         |                                                                                                                                                                                          |
|---------|------------------------------------------------------------------------------------------------------------------------------------------------------------------------------------------|
|         | a Catholic always a Catholic. Once a Protestant always a Prot …no always a bastard. No way you ever marry him St Peters or no St Peters.                                                 |
| Maggie  | Och Jimmy, she's young and he looked quite respectable looking boy.                                                                                                                      |
| Jimmy   | He's a Proddie and that's enough for me. They'll be no mixed marriages in the O'Hagan household and that's final. I don't want to hear another word about it. *Comprende*?               |
| Maggie  | But jimmy?                                                                                                                                                                               |
| Jimmy   | Never mind but Jimmy, I've said my piece and that's it. No more to be said. I'm off to bed! (He left and slammed the door behind him)                                                    |
| Maggie  | Mary, Mary, get up it's time for work. Mary, Mary?                                                                                                                                       |
| Maggie  | Jimmy Mary's gone, she's not in her room.                                                                                                                                                |
| Jimmy   | What do you mean not in her room?                                                                                                                                                        |
| Maggie  | I mean she's gone, not in her room what                                                                                                                                                  |

more do you need to know?

Jimmy: Where the hell has, she gone to? Maggie this is all your fault. You're too bloody soft with her. Gone because of you.

Maggie: My fault? I'd like to know where that came from Jimmy O'Hagan, don't you think you might; be responsible for this one?

Jimmy: Well you better bloody well find her, cause I'm not Havin' her marrying that Proddie scumbag, do you hear me?

Maggie: Yes, I hear you loud and clear Jimmy. But Mary's terrified of you and you're the one who's sent her away, and if she marries Wullie in a registry office or in a Protestant Church or even on the back of a bus, well good luck to her. You're a bigot Jimmy O'Hagan.

Jimmy: She's only bloody sixteen woman. Why the hell would they be talkin' marriage at that age anyway?

Maggie: If you'd have given the lad a chance to talk you might have known. Wullie has joined the navy, he gave Mary an engagement ring, and said they would wait till she was at least eighteen. I know that's still young, but if their love could last, William thought they would be ready to marry. The plan was he would stay in the Navy and he could get posted to Singapore with Mary if she was his wife. It would have been an extended honeymoon. You're too narrow-minded Jimmy. I'm off to bed.

**(In Wullie's house with his mum Betty and his dad Alex)**

| | |
|---|---|
| Wullie | Mary, what are you doing here? |
| Mary | I had to come Wullie, I can't stay in that house a moment longer. Do you think your mum and dad could put me up? |
| Wullie | I don't know Mary. Your dad was awful angry and if he finds out you're here with me. |
| Mary | I can't go back, please don't make me Wullie. |
| Betty | Mary you can stay here for the night, but you must go back to your parents, they will be worried about you. |
| Alex | Yes Mary Betty's right. You know you're welcome, but it wouldn't be right for us to keep you here, it would only make things worse. |

| | |
|---|---|
| Betty | Sleep on it dear and we'll have a wee word in the morning. |

**(Morning at Wullie's house)**

| | |
|---|---|
| Betty | Would you like some breakfast Mary? |
| Mary | That would be lovely Mrs McMillan, thanks. |
| Betty | Tell me Mary, your dad is Jimmy O'Hagan? Is that right? |
| Mary | Yes that's right Mrs McMillan, do you know my dad? |
| Betty | I knew your dad years ago Mary. Tell me how is your dad now? |
| Mary | Oh he must take a walk every day. He had a heart attack two years ago. He has to exercise every day. He walks in Kelvin Grove Park every day around ten o'clock. He's much better now, although he still needs to take it easy. He got very stressed when he met William. I wish he would get that bigoted trait he has out of his head. It's silly. |
| Betty | Did you know Mary that I'm a Catholic? |

|       |                                                                                                                                                                                                                                                                                                                                                                                       |
| ----- | ----------------------------------------------------------------------------------------------------------------------------------------------------------------------------------------------------------------------------------------------------------------------------------------------------------------------------------------------------------------------------------- |
|       | Did William not tell you?                                                                                                                                                                                                                                                                                                                                                           |
| Mary  | I Don't think Wull I mean William thinks like that Mrs McMillan. He was very shocked when he met my dad.                                                                                                                                                                                                                                                                            |
| Betty | We've never brought William up to have any prejudice, Mary. I was a Catholic and Alex was Protestant. I've a little secret, Mary. I was expecting William when I married Alex. My dad was just like yours. A total bigot when he found out I was expecting he threw me out. My mother was distraught. Alex and I married in the registry office, and we've been happy ever since. |
| Mary  | Oh that's a lovely story Mrs McMillan.                                                                                                                                                                                                                                                                                                                                              |
| Betty | Call me Betty Mary.                                                                                                                                                                                                                                                                                                                                                                 |
| Mary  | Okay, but that's a lovely story Betty. What happened with your mum and dad after you were married.                                                                                                                                                                                                                                                                                  |
| Betty | Well! My dad never spoke to me. But my mother did. She was very upset at what had happened. But after William was born my father came round and doted on his grandson. We made up, but sadly they've now both gone Mary. Go back home and think about things. You and William are                                                                                                  |

| | |
|---|---|
| | still very young. Make up with your dad. You're welcome here any time. |
| Mary | Thanks Mrs McMillan I mean Betty. I'll go home and see what happens but I'm not giving William up. We'll be married someday by hook or by crook. Chapel, Church or bus shelter I don't care. |

**(Mary's house)**

| | |
|---|---|
| Jimmy | And where do you think you've been young lady? |
| Mary | I stayed at Wullie's house last night. His parents are lovely. Not bigoted like you. His mum's a Catholic and she married his dad in a registry office because her dad was just like you and wouldn't hear tell of her marrying a Protestant, but she married him anyway, and they are really happy. I came home here because she told me to. Not because I want to. You don't need to worry about me running off to get married soon because Wullie's been posted to Plymouth to start his training in the Navy. But when he gets his next leave, I will be seeing him again with or without your permission. |

**(Jimmy out walking in the park)**

Jimmy        Betty Simpson. My God, I haven't seen you in years, yer as lovely as ever. What have you been up to all these years.

Betty        Hi Jimmy. Yes, I'm fine but I'm afraid we have a problem!

Jimmy.       A problem? How can we have a problem?

Betty.       Well for a start Jimmy this is not a chance meeting.

Jimmy.       What? How would you know where I would be at this time in the morning? I haven't set eyes on you for eighteen or is it nineteen years?

Betty        It's almost nineteen years jimmy. My son William is eighteen now.

Jimmy.       And why would you be meeting me to tell me that Betty?

Betty.       Well Jimmy my name is not Betty

Simpson now, it's Betty McMillan. Do you get the message, you're not just a bigot but a hypocrite into the bargain Jimmy O'Hagan?

Jimmy. So? William could be my son Betty? Yes, Jimmy that Protestant 'b' as you called him could be your son. Let's hope that him and Mary have not had an intimate relationship till I find out. I sincerely hope they have not. Not because they couldn't marry. But because I would not like William having your bigoted blood cruising through your body.

**(Betty walks off leaving a stunned Jimmy who eventually falls to the ground having a heart attack)**

**One year later. Glasgow dance hall**

| | |
|---|---|
| Wullie | Are ye dancin' |
| Mary | Are ye askin' |
| Wullie | I am askin' |
| Mary | Well am dancin' |

| | |
|---|---|
| Mary | Oh Wullie I've missed you so much. |
| Wullie, | I loved getting' yer letters Mary. |
| Mary | Me to Wullie. (giggles) I mean I loved getting' yours. |
| Wullie | I was sorry to hear about your dad Mary. I know he was an oul' bast I mean old bigot. What exactly happened to him? |
| Mary. | Well, he was out walking one day and he met an old friend. Ehh, I don't exactly know how to tell you this William, I didn't want to write and tell you, but this was what happened. He was out walking when as I said he bumped into an old friend. It was a lady friend. They got chatting. When I say old friend, I really mean old flame. Apparently, they were going to be married but she had met someone else. My mother told me that she had been the love of his life. However, this lady got up and married another man. When he bumped into her and they got talking, she told him she married a man called Alex McMillan. Has the penny dropped. He realised that she was your mother. Your mother and my father were lovers William. We could be brother and sister. |

|        |                                                                                                                                                                                 |
| ------ | ------------------------------------------------------------------------------------------------------------------------------------------------------------------------------- |
|        | Dad had a heart attack after your mother walked off leaving him stunned. It was awful. He's on the mend now.                                                                    |
| Wullie | Oh my God Mary. Just as well we never did anything. Do you mean that your dad could be my dad?                                                                                  |
| Mary   | That's exactly what I mean William. We need to get a DNA test otherwise it'll be brother and sister love.                                                                       |
| Wullie | What's your mother saying?                                                                                                                                                      |
| Mary   | She's in a state, but not as much as your mum and dad are William. Have they not said anything to you yet?                                                                      |
| Wullie | No, I just came to see you here. You told me in your letter this was where you would be. Oh, Mary, have you met anyone else in view of what you've just learned we could be related? |
| Mary   | No William, I'm just like you. I still love you, nothing's changed but we need those DNA tests.                                                                                 |
| Wullie | You're the wee Catholic Mary, get out those rosary beads and start praying. Where's your dad now?                                                                               |

| | |
|---|---|
| Mary | He's at home, we think he's on the mend; he has calmed down a lot. He wants to see you, William. |
| Wullie | I don't know Mary. Let's wait till after the D.N.A test are done, then maybe. We'll see. |
| Mary | That's fine Wullie I understand how you feel. |

**Mary Wullie Maggie, Betty and Alex in Betty and Alex' house**

| | |
|---|---|
| Wullie | Are ye goin' tae open the envelope ma? |
| Betty | (hands shaking) I'm scared. |
| Wullie | What do you think of all this da? I mean this has all come out because ma and Mary's da met up and they thought that Mary and I were lovers. Which we are not yet. Did you know that I might not be your son dad? |
| Alex | Your ma told me all about Jimmy O'Hagan, she had fallen out of love with him because of his prejudice. When she became pregnant, I knew you might not be mine, but I loved your mum, and that was that. And I love you. |

| | |
|---|---|
| Mary | Please Betty, open the results. I can't wait any longer |
| Betty | **(looking at Alex for a long time)** |
| Wullie | Oh for fuck's sake ma open the envelope. |
| Maggie | Please Betty open the envelope and put us all out of our misery. |
| Betty | **(Gingerly opening the envelope)** Alex! |
| Alex | I am going to say what Wullie said and you know I don't swear. Tell us what is In that fucking envelope? |
| Betty | Alex! William is **(long pause).** He's your son! |
| | **(All jumping up and down, hugging and kissing)** |
| Maggie | Calm down everyone we have a wedding to arrange. |

**Mary and William were Married in St Peters Catholic Church. Jimmy attended in a wheelchair.**

| | |
|---|---|
| Jimmy | I'm glad you're not my son William but proud to have you as my son in law and I |

| | |
|---|---|
| | would be honoured if you would call me dad. |
| Wullie | I have only one dad Jimmy, I'll just call you Jimmy if that's ok with you? |
| Jimmy | That'll do me fine son and I'm proud of you. I've learned a hard lesson and I realise life is far too short to bear grudges for nothing. In fact, this is the first time I've entered a chapel for I don't know how long. Who am I to preach about Catholics and Protestants? Have a lovely life together. |
| Wullie | Thanks Jimmy, I love Mary very much and I know we'll be very happy together. |

**At the reception.**

| | |
|---|---|
| William | I love you Mrs Mary McMillan |
| Mary | I love you too Mr William McMillan |
| William | Are ye dancin' |
| Mary | Are ye askin' |
| William | Aye am askin' |
| Mary | Then i'm dancing' |

**Band strikes up the first dance only sixteen**

| | |
|---|---|
| Wullie | Oor song dae ye know it |

| | |
|---|---|
| Mary | Shut up. Course I know it. |
| Wullie | I'm glad it's a Moonie. |

**THE END**

## AN ODE TO NANCY

We'll all miss oor Nancy pretty.

Glesga Toon wis her city

Nancy went to Barrowland

That great big ballroom was so grand.

Glitz and makeup to enhance.

Cause Nancy pretty loved to dance.

She then had Linda Wills and Peter

Her life could not get any sweeter.

Then her grandchildren and then great

How wonderful was her fate.

On the phone on Sunday nights

An hour chatting to Maggie.

Putting the world to rights.

Nancy, she did love to chatter.

Mags would listen to all her patter.

Down to Plymouth she would go.

Hated airports, found them her foe.

'Get assistance, 'we would say

Nance Would shout, 'piss off; no way.'

'A still can tackle a stair'.

Cause there's always a big boy there.'


At Tam and Mags on a Sunday

They would go Haybrook Bay

It was named the Haybrook walk

Tam would say, 'Nancy ye canny walk AND talk.

But oor gal did not give a monkey.

She could talk the hind legs aff a donkey.


Robert was her soul mate.

We all remember when they did date.

Maisie her mother called him T C

Everyone said, 'who is he?'

Oh, and just to fill in the gap.

T.C meant that chap.

They got wed in '87

Nancy thought she'd gone to heaven.

Robert was her one true love

She'll be caring for her Boab from above

Nancy, I don't have your life to a tee

But This story would not be complete.

Without mentioning your major heart surgery

So, to our Nancy a fond farewell

And lots of love from your wee pal Nell

Please raise your glass to our Nancy Pretty

I hope she liked this little ditty.

## NANCY'S TALE

My name is Nancy and I love to tell a story. Oh, just to let you know I can talk till the coos come hame. Well here goes. Me and ma Boab had booked to go on a river cruise. Ye, see I hate airports, so we were going on a coach trip to the Rhine. You know Glenton Coaches. We've been before. I always entertain awe the passengers about my major heart surgery, I love talking as long as it's about me. Anyway, to cut a long story short. Oh, I forgot I cannae but I'll try.

Ye see my family didn't want me to go on this trip because I was in hospital in March, I had double pneumonia and a collapsed lung, but I knew by August I'd be as fit as a butcher's dug. Even though my legs were all swollen; but the doctor sorted that out wae a massive doses of water tablets.

I was so looking forward to entertaining my fellow passengers with all the stories about me being in hospital. That along with my major heart surgery 12 years ago. Why did they all rush off the bus at coffee stops? Och, I know. It was so they could rush back on again and listen to me.

However, the best story is still to come. We got off the overnight ferry at Zeebrugge and got the coach to Cologne in Germany. That was On Sunday the 27th of

August 2017. Och my legs are a wee bit swollen I reiterated to my fellow passengers whom I knew were waiting on the latest episode of my illnesses.

We arrived at the river boat. It was lovely. We were on deck chatting and getting to know everyone. The food was great, although me and Boab don't have big appetites. Boab smokes like a chimney. Oh! I wonder if that has anything to do with my illness. Na!

However, we had a great night on Tuesday. I was singing my heid aff, would have loved to dance but my legs were a wee bit swollen. I went down to my cabin at aboot midnight. Boab said 'I'll no be long pet', he always called me pet. He was just having his last fag

I was reading my book and fell asleep, and guess what happened????? I never woke up again. Yes, that's right...... I went and died, how's that for a story. My fellow passengers will dine out on that one for a long time.

Poor wee Boab found me at 5 in the morning. I was still alive at one when he came down. My family had a nightmare getting me home. I was sorry about that. That's another story that unfortunately I cannae tell.

I must go, St Peter's waiting at the gates anxious to hear all my stories. Just as well I've got eternity to tell them. Tara see you all when it's your turn.

Lots of love from Nancy.

## MY PHOBIA

We walked in together. 'You'll be fine I'll be with you and hold your hand' he said! I'd always known there was a cruel streak in him, but on this occasion, I trusted him. How wrong I was. Just as the doors were beginning to close, he jumped out. I screamed, 'no please, please don't do this,' but here I was all alone in my worst nightmare. Stuck in an elevator.

We had come to New York to try and patch up our relationship. Booked a penthouse in a hotel on the 50th floor. I was a bit wary when he booked, I am claustrophobic, hated lifts but he reassured me that he would be with me.

How was I going to survive this ordeal? I closed my eyes and thought, these lifts go up quickly then I felt a shudder, all the lights went out and the lift stopped. I screamed for help but nothing, I fumbled in my bag for my mobile, no signal. I screamed again and again till I had no voice, slid down the wall. I thought I'm going to have a heart attack, then passed out. How long I was in there I don't know.

There was another great shudder, and the light was on. The doors opened at the penthouse and there he was grinning like a Cheshire cat. I was still on the floor and pleaded hoarsely get me out.

He laughed as he pulled me free. I stumbled into the apartment shaking and in total shock.

He looked around the room mesmerized. This is not the apartment I asked for. 'It is beautiful' I said. A stunning terrace with tremendous views over Manhattan. I opened the French doors and stepped out. He screamed, 'close those doors. I booked an apartment with a window, not a terrace.' I needed fresh air but did as he said as usual and came inside.

He visibly relaxed and opened a bottle of champagne then another and another, laughing uncontrollably he shouted, 'I engineered the elevator stopping and the power cut just to teach you a lesson.'

I studied him closely and realised he fears heights. We drank our champagne. Me less than him. I could see he was getting drunk. I opened the terrace door and coaxed him out. The champagne had gone to his head. He gingerly stepped on to the terrace. Quickly I closed and locked the door and put the key into my pocket.

No no he screamed. 'Now you know how I feel you cowardly bastard.' He wrestled with me to try and get the keys and hadn't realised how near he was to the edge. He was very drunk. It was easy to gently tip him over, hear him scream as he soared down to splatter on Broadway.

I left the apartment my fear of the elevator was gone. It took all of two minutes to reach the foyer. I stepped out to the lullaby of Broadway. Police sirens screaming, a gruesome crowd milling around a flattened dead body, blood everywhere. I was now free in New York. Claustrophobia gone. Or was it? Next hotel will be on the ground floor. Fuck the lift and the view.

## CAREFUL PLANNING

I stormed out banging the door, well; more like taking it off its hinges. The cheek of him telling me his shirt was wrinkled. I'd taken all bloody day ironing.

'Well, it matches your face' I said as I banged the door. I was seething, nothing I did pleased him. No wonder I take a drink, that's another thing. It's okay for him to come home from the pub legless, but not me. Oh no! I was not allowed. He would slur when I had a drink. 'I shee you you've got a glass in your hand.' 'ha!' I'd say, 'I take it, it's a case of do as I say not as I do.' Feckin' cheek of him.

Well, here I am, pondering. Seven years we've been married. I think he must have the seven-year itch. I wish someone would scratch it till it bloody well bleeds.

I'm standing on the beach not far from our little remote cottage. We thought we'd be so happy here, maybe a few children to bring up. But it wasn't to be. He blamed me. I had all the tests. There was nothing wrong, but the big macho man wouldn't go. Oh no it couldn't be him. Our marriage deteriorated over the years.

I was staring over the sea; it was only seven in the morning. He was going to a conference allegedly. I was reflecting on our seven-year marriage. Was I happy? Not really. I know what I'll do; I'll kill myself. Yes! I'll just stroll into the sea and drown. That'll teach them.

I can just imagine when they find my body all washed up like a beached whale, swollen and distorted. His mother the hypocrite, wailing, howling, and bawling with her crocodile tears. His reprobate father trying to console her; and my seven-year husband bending over me crying his eyes out saying I wish I'd treated her better. It was all over that shirt this morning. That'll teach them I smirked to myself, thinking how clever my plan was.

Oh! Wait a minute, maybe It wasn't such a good plan, I wouldn't be there to witness it. Perhaps they wouldn't be bawling their eyes out. They might be glad to see the back of me. In fact, they probably would.

I know what I'll do. I'll do a Lord Lucan, or a Reggie Perrin. Fake my own death. Yes, that's exactly what I'll do. In fact, I'll do it now.

I took all my clothes off to leave on the beach for evidence and stood there stark naked, then I had second thoughts, the tide will come and take them away and also where in the hell can I go starkers.

This needs careful planning. I'll come back tomorrow with a change of clothes, put the other ones on the rocks where the tide can't reach and take the money where my crook of a husband has his secret plank, that's not really a secret, because I know where it is. Yes, planning is what's needed.

I started to scramble into my clothes when I heard a dog barking, there was a woman with the dog they were approaching quickly. I managed to grab my cardigan, looked around frantically. I saw a big rock and behind it was a small cave, I just managed to reach it before they saw me.

I ran behind the rock struggling into my cardigan, shrank back as far as I could into the little space the cave provided. The cardigan barely covered my belly button, oh God what am I to do? This is all his fault, and his pathetic mother and father, thick as thieves they are, the bastards.

The woman and the dog approached. The dog ran right up to my clothes and had a good old sniff. Oh no! He's going to rip all my clothes to pieces. The woman said something to the dog, looked at my clothes and then stared out to sea for a few minutes. It was obvious what was on her mind.

Meanwhile the dog having got the scent from my clothes decided to come round and have a little sniff at me huddled behind the rock. 'Shoo' I said, he was trying to lick my face. 'Go away you scrawny beast,' I whispered in my most menacing whisper.

I peeked out and saw the woman coming my way. I shrank back into my hidey hole as far as I could. The dog lost interest and then I heard the woman shouting at him and he scampered after her. I peeked round the rock making ready to run for my clothes but the inevitable happened. The woman had them firmly tucked under her arm.

I sat there with my cardigan pulling it round me as far as it would go, as I said it barely covered me. There were more people now meandering on the beach as it was getting later, then everyone seemed to disappear, and I realised why.

Plop, plop, plop heavier and heavier. Although I was in the little cave the wind was blowing the rain in. I pulled my cardigan over my head but the rest of me was completely naked. I was shivering and cold and my tears mingled with the rain.

I thought of my nice cosy little house. What was I going to do? Then I heard it! Sirens. Oh shit! In minutes the beach was swarming with police. Obviously, the woman had taken my clothes to them.

I listened to their talking and looking out to sea, the next thing I heard was, "Hack, hack, hack, a bloody helicopter was hovering over the sea. A line was being dropped down with a diver, and then another. Should I give myself up? I'll go to jail for wasting police time. Why did I think up this stupid idea? I don't want to go to jail but what was the alternative?

I was just about to go out naked and give myself up when I heard voices I recognised. It was my husband, his mother and father. My bag had been on the beach with my identity in it; the police had informed them of what they had discovered.

I was absolutely terrified. I'll just shout and let them know where I am and ask them to bring something to cover me up. Just as I was about to come clean, I heard my mother-in-law say. 'What a stupid bitch, what was she trying to prove? Did you tell her about your affair?'

Affair? What bleedin' affair? I never knew of any affair. 'Don't be so stupid mother, why would I tell her about that, but the stupid little bitch has made it easy for me now. Hasn't she,' he sneered.

Then it hit me! Here I was really faking my own death and hearing what they thought of me. I cowered back into the tiny cave and thought what will I do now. I was frozen, wet, and tired.

I waited till dark, pondering. A plan was forming. Thank goodness my cardigan had dried. I still had my watch, I really thought I was going to die with hypothermia. It was two in the morning,

I sneaked out of my hiding place, tied my cardigan round the bottom half of me giving me a little modesty, crossed my arms over my chest.

I was so stiff from crouching in the same position it took me a while to straighten. I looked all around, there was not a soul in sight.

I crept back in the dark shadows. It was the early hours of Saturday morning; he would be in a drunken stupor by now. Thank the Lord the door was unlocked. Stupid drunken bastard wouldn't think to lock the door.

I tiptoed in, went straight to the bedroom, there he was just as I knew he would be, sprawled out stark naked on the bed. His jacket was lying over the chair. I put on some gloves and searched in his pockets and took out all the money he had. Then I rummaged and found his mobile phone. He was still dead to the world.

I scrolled down his mobile messages and found what I was looking for. 'Sorry I can't make it tonight darling, but I'll make it up to you tomorrow, if you know what I mean. Purr, purr.' I promptly deleted all the messages she had sent him.

The barmaid from the pub. The dyed blond, buxom, painted whore bitch. How dare he choose her over me. I was devoured with rage. I'll purr feckin' purr you. Lucky you couldn't make it tonight bitch.

I checked my desk and yes it was there. Then I went to the place that was a secret but wasn't a secret. I lifted out all the money, I would count that later I knew it would be north of a quarter of a million.

Then the piece de resistance, his little revolver. Ha! If only he guessed. I lifted out the gun; I knew he always kept it loaded just in case some of his crook pals came calling with a menacing attitude.

I lifted it out carefully, held it away from me. I had never in my life touched a gun. I tiptoed into the bedroom where he still lay in the same position snoring his little old' head off. Not for long my beauty.

I lifted his hand, he grunted a little, I froze for a moment then I wrapped his fingers round the gun placing his forefinger on the trigger and pulled. All his hopes and dreams spilled onto the pillow. I felt nothing. Not even sick. We were lucky that our cottage was so remote. No one would hear a sound.

I dressed in what clothes I needed for the journey, tied a headscarf round my head and walked from the house forever.

I walked about two miles, then got a taxi. I was glad he was a grumpy driver and didn't want to chat. He hardly noticed me. He dropped me about a mile from the airport, I would walk the rest, didn't want the taxi driver to know I was going to the airport. I was glad I had ready money. We never really used banks due to my crook husband; there would be no paper trail. There was no problem getting through security with my fake passport, 'just in case of an emergency' he would say. Well, this was certainly an emergency. My real passport was in my desk that I had checked earlier. Faking my own death was much easier than I thought. All my clothes were in the cottage, my real passport and as I said no paper trail. The joys.

I sat on the lovely Caribbean beach, sipping a cold long cocktail, listening to a lovely steel band playing behind me. I had a million pounds stashed.

Thoughts of the other beach I'd left behind came to mind. I had no regrets.

I had managed to get hold of a British newspaper.

**Headlines:**

**'Woman drowns herself in the sea.**

**Husband shoots himself in grief.**

**Case closed.'**

**Who says crime doesn't pay!**

## MY FAVOURITE SONG

My favourite song

Now let me see.

It was Wee Willie Winky

When I was three.

Then came the teenage years,

Many songs left me in tears.

The Beatles and the Rolling Stones

How I loved their dulcet tones.

I Can't Get No Satisfaction,

The whole dance floor leapt into action.

Help came via

John, Paul, George and Ringo,

Love me do was their first single.

Abba then came on the scene.

The whole world were

Singing Dancing Queen

Ach I've gone all hazy.

Patsy Cline is driving me Crazy.

Then the old songs come to mind

Danny boy and Auld Lang Syne

Och I've thought so long I'm weary,

So, I hope you don't find my song dreary.

I'll sing the chorus of my favourite song,

If you know it please sing along.

Let me tell you that I love you,

That I think about you all the time

Caledonia, you're calling me

Now I'm going home.

But if I should become a stranger

It would make me more than sad.

Caledonia's been everything I've ever had.

## MA MAMMY

Where's ma school bag Mammy?

Sannie, yer dae'n ma heid in a swear.

A canny find it Mammy,

Oh! There it's there.

Can a go oot tae play Mammy?

Aye but remember come hame fur yer tea.

Gonnie let me in Mammy?

Am bustin' fur a pee.

Don't want tae go tae bed Mammy.

Don't gie me awe that grief.

Ach! Can a read ma book Mammy?

Naw! go an clean yer teeth.

Whit ur ye dae'n Sannie?

Ach am jist squeezin' a pluke.

Year gien me the boak Sannie

A think am gonnie puke.


Am gaun oan a date Mammy.

Who is she son?

She's big Lizzie fae the Calton.

Whit? Her that weighs a ton?


She gied me a dissy Mammy.

 She didn'ae son awe naw.

She be'ter no come near me Sannie

Cause' a'll gie her a belt roon the jaw.


A goat another date Mammy.

Awe that's great son.

Her name is Jeannie Mammy.

Aye.  An' she's the wan.

Yer gaunie be a granny Mammy.

Oh, son am o'er the moon.

A canny wait Mammy

The wean.  It'll be here soon.


Wur cawin' her Lulu Mammy.

Whit kin a name is that?

It's efter the singer Mammy.

Whit? That screechin' brat?


Ach she's fair grown-up Sannie.

Aye she's already goat two teeth.

She's in 'tae everything Mammy

Aye ye need eyes in the back o' yer heid.


Ach a loved ye Mammy

A hate tae see ye go.

We did everything the gether,

So wae tears its cheerio.

A'll never forget ye Mammy

Yer the best that ever wis.

So, frae yer son, Wee Sannie

A send ye a great big kiss.

**IS IT HAUNTED?**

It was on a Monday morning,

I tiptoed down the stair.

Thought that I'd heard voices.

But there was no one there.

I stepped inside the parlour,

It felt extremely strange.

A big glass box was standing

Where there used to be the range.

This is where the voices came,

People moved inside it.

I stood rooted to the spot.

Was completely astounded.

Were they hiding at the back?

I peeked round to see.

But again, to my shock.

There was only me.

I nearly jumped out of my pelt.

When an object gave a ping.

It danced around the table.

Then it began to sing.

Oh, dear I think I'm going mad.

Or am I being taunted?

My house? It needs exorcised.

Because I think it's haunted.

I then hear voices from the lawn.

A family having tea.

It is then I realise.

The Ghost? Well!! It is me.

## DAE YE REMEMBER?

Ye might no' know what I'm talkin' aboot
If yer 50 or 60 or aulder tae boot
Sit back in yer chair if ye'll just hear me oot
But ye might no remember?"

The steamie the washoose that wis roon the back
Boilers, wally sinks that aye had a crack.
A board that ye scrubbed claiths that were grey,
They were used in skiffle groups
Where teenagers would sway.
Dae ye remember?

Wally closes that were scrubbed till they shone.
The leerie who lit the gas lamps until dawn,
Oot playing in the street till ye needed a wee
When ye didn'ae want tae go hame fur yer tea.


The sunshine that lasted all through the day.
Glauber mud pies made wae watter and clay,
Peever, ropes and hunch cuddy hunch
A puddy up, but there was nae lunch.

Cause there were pieces thrown from above,
Wae sugar, jam and jeely and a whole lot of love.
We went tae the pictures on a Saturday
Where Roy Rogers and Trigger were in the matinee.

We sat in oor seats and shouted so loud,
Thrown sweeties and caramels into the crowd.
Comin' oot like cowboys slappin' oor bums,
With pretend horses, oor fingers were guns.

The shoap that sold ye sweets fur a penny,
Way back then there must have been many.
Fish and chips oan a Friday a must
A wee swally fur daddy tae quench his thirst.

A pokey hat fur the weans and nugget for mammy,
Ye would get them from the café
That was owned by the Tally.
We played wee shoaps broken glass for the money,
Sellin' sweeties and crisps and the odd jar of honey.
Awe made wae mud and paper in bits
That was torn up fur the fish and the chips.

The man wae the barra would always come roon.
Blawin' his bugle that was aye oot o' tune,
Fur some smelly claiths ye got a balloon.
Then ye would listen tae awe his auld gags,
And he'd go on his way shoutin TOYS FOR RAGS.

The back court talent they sang their hearts oot
For some scalding hot pennies as they bellowed for loot.
Objects would come from some flats on the top
Dishes, wet cloots and the occasional mop.
They ducked and they dived but they wouldn't stop.

We made oor ain fun, I would have to say.
Nae computers or lap tops were there fur tae play.
Nae telly at night tae sit doon and watch,
We'd rether be oot playing hopscotch.
The wireless, piano were there at oor back
But we'd sit roon the table enjoying the craic.

Wee rooms and kitchens nae lavvies inside,
Single ends and lobbies where people did bide.

Big grey tenements reaching up to the sky,
Horrible buildings where people would die.

It was so glowing when you were wee,
Glasgow the green place was ever so twee.
But would you really like to go back?
Tae nae telly or mod cons that oor grannies did lack.

I really don't know if I could live like that noo,
Where always the sky was so bright and blue.
When summers would last from June till September
But I am so pleased that I can remember.

## THE BLUEBELL WOODS

The bluebell woods up in the Drum

Was where I ventured with my chum.

Hide and seek behind the trees.

Amid the wildlife

Wae skint knees.

Ma Mammie asks?

Were you in that bluebell forest?

Naw Mamie, I lie; honest!

A cannae tell her we were there

Because she told me to beware

Of bad men hingin' aboot,

And if I was lying, I'd get a cloot.

We went back the very next morn,

Was feart tae go hame

'Cause ma claithes were awe torn.

I tiptoed up the stair,

Heard her shout, is that you there?

She looked at me wae distaste

An angry frown upon her face.

But then, on her lips a smile did crack.

When I produced a bunch of bluebells

That I'd hidden behind my back.

## MY FIRST KISS

I remember my first kiss; it was bloody awful. My pal and myself were on a bus run to Helensburgh. Yes, that's right Helensburgh. I lived in Drumchapel so Helensburgh was a fair journey. I was fifteen at the time.

Susan had been kissed several times, but me never. I looked young for my age, pigtails didn't help. Only joking, not at fifteen.

There were two boys on the bus about our age. They were playing guitars and singing Beatles songs. I named them good looking and ugly. Obviously, I fancied good looking, but he only had eyes for Susan. When I say eyes for Susan, I really mean Susan's boobs. They were enormous. She always got the guys.

The two boys latched on to us. good looking with Susan and ugly with me. To be fair he wasn't ugly I just fancied good looking.

Immediately Susan started snogging good looking, and I started snogging ugly. I found it very awkward and didn't know how to cope. But since I'd never been kissed. I mean I was fifteen for goodness' sake. So, when the boy sat beside me I thought what the hell. My first kiss I've never forgotten. I'll tell you why It was bloody rotten.

His lips were all slobbery. I was glad to get off the bus at Helensburgh, determined I would not kiss him on the way back. Once we were off the bus the guys disappeared. It was a lovely day. We bought fish and chips in Dino's Café, eating them on a seat looking over the estuary.

As we were heading back a great big seagull shat on Anne's head. I started to laugh but she obviously did not find it amusing. She went into the public toilet to try and clean it off, but her hair looked a mess. I wondered what good looking will think of her now?

We got on the bus, and I found a seat by myself well away from ugly, but good looking didn't notice Ann's messy shitty hair. His eyes were where they were before, on her great big mammaries. I fell asleep while Susan snogged good lookin' all the way back to the Drum.

I vowed never again would I kiss a guy I didn't fancy. You'd have thought I'd have learned a lesson, but vanity is a powerful deadly sin.

I was at the pictures one night with my pal Catherine. Catherine thought she was God's gift. Two boys came over to chat us up. They were ok, however Catherine decided she would have the handsome one. I didn't rate either, but the so-called handsome one only had eyes for me, so to spite her I decided to get off with him. Wrong decision.

Oh my God I had forgotten!

I nearly fainted.

His breath was rotten.

My first kiss

It was a miss

Would you share

Your first kiss?

## THE PLAN

Andrew had a plan! 'Don't be silly It'll never work.' I said. 'Have you seen the state of the world Mary?' 'What you have in mind is outrageous, not the answer.'

'We need to plan the route. You faint, nobody will notice me.' 'It is too dangerous Andrew.' 'Mary, I have not served in the army for nothing, I know exactly what I'm doing.'

'We could get the death penalty for what you are about to do.' 'Many people may get the death penalty if I don't do it. All you must do is faint. Tomorrow! Mary, It's our only chance.'

Up at the crack of dawn, we checked the map and newspapers. The parade was due at eleven prompt.

We were there at nine to secure a place at the front. Music was playing and there was a cheery, festive atmosphere. We saw the cavalcade approach. Andrew stole into the shadows. I pretended to faint, distract attention.

Andrew emerged. He could clearly see the man's golden floppy hair, he was waving and smiling in his false ingratiating way.

The silver gun glistened. The man's golden hair turned red. Having played his 'TRUMP' card, Andrew stole back into the crowd.

## LOVE HURTS

Wullie: What year were you born?

Katie: 2000

Wullie: That was the same year I was

born. We're millennials

Wullie, I've no seen you for years. A always fancied you Katie

Katie A know. A always fancied you too.

Wullie: It's a pity we never got together back then. We were so suited. Liked the same things. I cannae believe it; it's 2080! Awe they year's Katie. Wee millennium kids fancied each other awe these years ago and it never really came to anything. A wee fumble maybe?

Katie: Ach a know how ye feel Wullie I feel the same. Did you find it sore Wullie?

Wullie: A wee bit. I think it was sorer fur you than it wis fur me.

Katie: So, does yours look the same? Can I see it?

Wullie: Naw, it's awe wrinkly and blue. Can I see yours?

Katie : Naw mine's awe wrinkly and rid and fiery. Like a volcano.

Wullie: Wis it no awful whit we did back then when ye think aboot it. We didn't think how wrinkled they both would get.

Katie Mines awe wizened an definitely dis'ne look the same. Anybody who sees it just cringes. A cover it up awe the time.

Wullie: A know Katie I'm the same. But it was the style back then. Like it or lump it. No matter what age ye are 85 90 yer tattoos were always gonnie get wrinkly wan day. But it was the style back then.

## YE BANKS AND BRAES O' CLYDEBANK TOON

### (To the tune of Ye banks and braes)

Ye banks and braes

O' Clydebank Toon

Kilbowie Road

Runs up and doon

Ye built the Queen's

And sewing machines

The river Clyde

Is in your genes

*CHORUS*

Oh Clydebank Toon

Nae horns at noon.

Nae bustling crowds

On Glesga Road

But your history

Will for ever run.

But sadly never

To Return.

There was John Brown's yard.

And Singers too

And the famous launch

Of the QE 2

But that was back

In '67

When Clydebank Toon

Was in seventh heaven.

CHORUS

## THE KINGS ABDICATION

Bella: did ye hear the news oan
the radio that the king
is abdicating?

Jessie: Aye! That's awful, but he
want's to marry the woman
He loves.

Bella: A know. It's wan load o' shite.
a cannae go that Wallis.
Whit the hell does he see
in her. She's as ugly as fuck.

**Two day's later. Jessie rapping on Bella's door.**

Jessie: Bella, Bella did you hear
the news? The King's no
abdicating. Parliament
has given him a reprieve
so he's going to be King
after all.

Bella: So you're telling me that
ugly American divorced
cow is gonnie be Queen?

Jessie: Aye, that's what am telling ye.

**1st September 1939. war breaks out.**

Bella: Oh Jessie, we're awe
doomed. See the King?
He's in cahoots wae that

Hitler wan. If he wins the war we'll be Sprechen du Deutsch.

Jessie: Sperchen du Whit? Yer no makin' sense?

Bella: Speaking German ya silly cow.

Jessie: Ach how am I supposed to know that? I think you're becoming a traitor.

Bella: You know nothing. Am telling you, that Hitler fella will change oor language tae German. Believe you me.

Jessie: We'll awe need tae go tae Night classes or that bloody Monster will send us to The gas chambers.

**1945 war over**

Bella: Thank God for Winston Churchill if it wisn'ae for Him that King would have Had us awe Sprechen Du Deutsch. No two ways About it.

Jessie: Is Dutch no Holland?

Bella: No! Dautschland is Germany. Not Dutch Deutsch.

Jessie: A always thought douche Wis something to dae wae Washing yersel' doon Below? Like giving yersel' A good auld douche.

Bella: Ach there's nae Educating You Jessie. Yer just a Numpty. Whit school did you Go tae? The dafty School.

Jessie: Shut it you. Yer no so clever Yersel'.

Bella: Anyway! We won the war, Thank God. We can awe get oan wae oor lives noo.

## 28th May 1972 Bella banging on Jessie's door. Singing

Bella. Ding dong the King Is dead God save our gracious King

Jessie: Whit are you fuckin' oan about noo?

Bella: A just heard it oan the news King Eddie's deid.

Jessie: So, who's the King noo?

Bella: I think it's Lizzie's son Charlie.

Jessie: So????????9 Who's Lizzie and who's Charlie?

Bella: Oh! Fur fucks sake Jessie Lizzie is Princess Elizabeth the daughter of George who was the King's brother. The wan that would have Become King if Edward had abdicated. A think that's why they gave Eddie a reprieve 'cause George stuttered like Fuck. Anyway Charles is Elizabeth's son and I think in line of succession Eddie had nae weans and George is deid The Succession goes to the male Heir who is Charles. He's Just 23.

Jessie: Awe that's nice

**28th July 1981. King Charles 111 and Lady Diana Spencer's Wedding**

Jessie: Is she no just lovely? does this mean that

Diana will be Queen?

Bella: Aye! That's what it means Jessie. She's a lovely wee lassie, but they've just picked her 'cause she's,a virgin.

Jessie: How in the fuck dae they know that? Have they been lookin' up her ying yang?

Bella: Aye probably. They cannae have the King marrying used goods. A feel sorry fur her. He's about 11 years aulder. Don't think she knows whit she's gettin' into. I think he's still shaggin' that Camilla wan?

Jessie: Is that the horsey lookin' cow? Hope she never becomes Queen?

Bella: Naw! That'll never happen. She's just the spare oan the side. Diana's the Queen.

**Fast forward 21st June 1982**

Bella: That's King Charles and Queen Diana had a wee boy. They've named him William.

Jessie: Awe that's lovely. Does that mean he'll become King when Charles pops his clogs?

Bella: Aye! That's what it means Jessie. Another King Billy.

Jessie: Awe! Fur fucks sake. We're surely no gaun doon that road again?

Bella: Afraid so Jessie. Afraid so.

**The End**

## A KNIFE THROUGH MY HEART

I told my kids when I'm dead

Put a knife through my heart!

Absolutely not they said

Don't think that would be smart.

I should have gone to the crem

That would have been wise.

I would have known I'd be dead

And wouldn't hear their cries.

But no I booked a plot

Up in yonder sound

What if I'm still alive

When they put me in the ground

Should I change my venue?

Ash or bones to choose.

No matter what the outcome

I'm still about to lose.

Being claustrophobic

Makes my life a pain.

Hope when I die

I don't die in vain.

So, when you think I'm dead

Put a knife Through my heart.

I said to my kids.

It really would be smart.

## ALL HALLOWS EVE

It was All Hallows Eve

A creepy time of year

A time of horror

A time of fear

Anything fur wur Halloween Missus?

I took them in

They sang their song

Would not be long

They'd soon be gone.

They were dressed.

All sorts of wear

Some were funny

Some to scare.

They shouted trick or treat?

So, I gave them all a sweet

Is that awe we get for our wee song?

I looked at them.

YES! They'd soon be gone.

I kissed them all on their neck

Their blood was sweet

It was just a peck.

They followed me into my cellar

No need to be out in this cold weather.

Their little faces filled with fear

They will sleep until next year.

Next year came next year dawned

More trick or treaters to be spawned.

Halloween it comes too often

Just want to snuggle in my coffin.

The doorbell rang all Hallows Eve

More trick or treaters to deceive.

Anything fur wur Halloween missus?

I took them in, they sang their song

Would not be long.

They'd soon be gone.

Some were funny some were tarty

They be ready for next years party

## DIFFERENT WORLDS

Birds with their wings

Flying in the sunlight

The lazy cat sleeping by the door.

Allowing the birds their freedom

Roof tops glistening with snow

Smoke billowing

From tall chimney pots

Cows chewing the cud

That the farmer

Had brought from the silo

A meandering river

Gurgling, enjoying

It's sleepy way to the sea.

Milk maids in clogs

Setting about their daily toil

Ample wife indoors

Cooking delights for the day

Buttermilk scones

Treats she knew

Was the way to her husband's heart?

Dogs playing in the yard

Barking and growling

At unwanted strangers.

Trees, their arms waving

In a gentle breeze

Creating a noise

Both musical and calming

Men toiling the soil.

Eating from its gifts

Enjoying the food of life

A world without malice

How wonderful

\*\*\*

Ragamuffins rummaging

In polluted bins

Beggars, street urchins and pickpockets.

Servants, whom the rich treated

Like the growling dogs

In the farmyard.

A ring of roses they sang

Cholera, dysentery, diphtheria

Dying children

Clinging to their mother's empty breast

For succour they could not claim.

No phones or mobiles

To spoil their peace

No computers

No social network to rob their privacy

No cars to polluted their precious air

No planes.

No continental treats

No N.H.S

## THE PHONE CALL

Have you ever felt distraught?

When you're on the phone

To be spoken to by robots

With a flattened tone?

Your call is important.

We'll be with you soon.

Then my eardrums nearly burst

By a great big rocking tune

The music stops I'm through at last

I sigh with relief.

Then the robots back

Your call is important. Oh no

It begs beyond belief.

Half an hour has gone by

Robots, music I just want to die.

Then at last a human voice

I have to listen there is no choice.

The voice is clear it does sound grand

But the accent I cannot understand.

Then I'm told the department's wrong

Hold the line, listen to the song.

Now I'm back to square one

Hearing again the robot's tone.

I F and blind, I swear and curse.

The robot states

Your call will be recorded

For a training purpose.

I can't believe it I have to scoff

But before I leave. I shout.

**FUCK OFF**

## HEAD TO TOE

I remember when

I'd long brown hair

That shimmered down my back.

It is still brown with a little help

From L'Oréal in a pack.

Now I must come to my eyes

They were always so bright.

Then came the cataracts

That dimmed my bloody sight.

I remember when my flesh was taught

And swimming was a breeze.

Now my costume's tightened

'Cause my boobs

Have reached my knees.

I used to wear a summer dress

Without the straps and strings.

Now I have to cover up

To hide my bingo wings.

Then there's the belly

What more can I say

The Children came along

'Cause he had his wicked way.

Going down to my pins

They were firm to my delight.

But no more I'm afraid

That damned cellulite.

To my feet my tiny toes

They danced the night away

Then corns and bunions came along

Much to my dismay.

So why do we have to age?

It is a crying shame

I wish there was a pill

So, we all could stay the same.

## THE WONDERFUL BAY

**(Tune to the song of the Clyde)**

There is a wee pub in

Bowling so dear

You can sit and relax

Have a wine or a beer.

They'll offer you coffee

Hot chocolate or tea

And it sits near the Clyde

That wynds down to the sea.

**Chorus**

Oh! The Bay the Bay

The wonderful Bay

They'll welcome you in

Any time of the day

It's a cosy wee inn

What more can I say

The Bay the Bay

The wonderful Bay.

There's Kirstin and Tina

And Vicky so fair

But they'll no lift

Ye up if ye up if ye fa' oan the flair.

So be careful what ye swally

And don't drink no more

Or ye might find yersel'

Flung right oot the door.

**Chorus**


There's Johnny Mulrine

And Cathy's there too.

There's Frazer and Jack

And they're awe gettin' fu'

When Kirstin' decides

To bang on her gong

The whole of the pub

Just bursts into song.

**Chorus**

So good luck to Kirsten

And all of her crew.

What in the hell would

We do without you?

We'd have to leave Bowling

And go to O K.

So remember you punters

To frequent the Bay.

## WORD POWER

Your just stupid my father said

As he threw my maths across the floor

I knew then I'd come to nothing

And bolted out the door.

I grew up and got a job

Very boring work

What else could I do

I was just a stupid jerk.

One day I realised

My dad was very wrong

I knew I wasn't stupid

Then burst into song

Gave up my boring job

With such joy and glee

Went off to college

Got myself a degree.

The power of that word stupid

Had caused me so much strife.

Never call anybody stupid

It could end someone's life.

Now know I'm not

A CUPID STUNT at last;

So, I challenge all of you

To say that one fast?

## YE KNOW YE KNOW

Ma names Wullie ye know, I live in a wee basement in the Gallowgate.

It's rented ye know, A don't work, well, a sometimes help in a stall doon the Barra's ye know. Anyway, the sun was oot the other day ye know, so I decided to pull out an auld deck chair that the landlord had Left me ye know, there a wis sunnin' masel in the basement space outside ma windae ye know, when this wee drunk bachle decided tae stick his willie through the railings and pish all over me. A wis drooket ye know. The wee bastard then staggered on his way and he didn'ae even know what he'd done ye know.

***drooket*** (Soaked through)

***Bachle*** (Untidy or clumsy person)

***Barra's*** (Place in Glasgow where second hand goods were sold from Barrows)

## I AM NEITHER

I am neither a boy nor a girl

My head well it's all in a swirl

You'll either loath me or love me

What I am, well just wait and see.

Nobody listens.

I have a story to tell

So, I just retreat

Right Into my shell.

Don't judge me

Please give me a chance

You may even like me

If you're in France

Look at me closer

I won't bite

I'm just a wee snail

An hermaphrodite.

No gender I have.

So please don't be coy

You see what I mean.

Neither a girl nor a boy.

## JACK

There was a Labrador

He was big and black.

The best dog ever

His name was Jack


Fraser was his daddy

Took him up the Humphrey hill.

Jack, he just loved it

He thought it was brill


Jack had a mummy

Her name was Val.

Rayne was her husky

And she was Jack's pal


Jacks' 12$^{th}$ birthday

Was spent in the Bay

He was one of the punters

What more can I say

Sadly, Jacks legs were done
And we had to say goodbye.
We all loved him
There was not a dry eye

Jack is now in heaven
With his sister Rayne
We will never forget you Jack
I'm sure we'll meet again.

## THE BUTCHERCRATIC OATH

There was not a mark, it was a shame to let it lie there, had it died in vain? I went to look, thought it might still be alive, but the poor thing was dead. Its bushy tail spread out like a fan.

I couldn't leave this beautiful creature who had been alive just minutes before, hated the thought of him being squashed under the numerous cars that would be passing soon. I lifted him; jeez he was heavy, opened the boot of the car with the remote, heaved him in, never really thinking what I would do with him.

At home my Wife Laura was cooking dinner, my tummy rumbled with the aroma wafting out from the kitchen. 'That smells delicious. What are we having tonight?' 'Posh stew,' Laura laughed. 'Boeuf bourguignon. In other words, beef stewed with wine and shallots.'

After dinner I took her out and opened the boot. 'God Angus, what *are* you doing with him?' She gasped! 'We'll place him in our large Freezer.' I said. After watching a TV program about roadkill. I asked Laura. 'Could you eat Mr Fox?' Screwing her face in disgust she said. **'Absolutely not.'**

I'd forgotten all about Mr Fox. After the discussion about eating him. Laura said 'Angus we should take Mr fox out of the freezer and bury him?'

Next day we lifted Mr Fox out of the freezer. He was even heavier than before with him being frozen, dumped him in the boot of the car along with the shovel to bury him; I thought of the programme about eating roadkill and promptly changed direction to our local butcher.

'Hi Sam' I smiled as I entered. 'Ello Angus me lad, what can I do for you?' 'Can I show you what I have in my car Sam?' Sam walked out with me, I was apprehensive about opening the boot, but thought it's now or never, I popped the boot open, and Sam looked inside. 'Right, me lad I take it you want him butchered. It's all the rage son.' He laughed. 'I'll have to have a look at him first, can't have you poison yourself.'

I told him he was still warm when I found him and there was no visible blood. 'But Angus, it could be the innards. I'll check him over and if he's ok, I'll go ahead and butcher him for you and give you a ring? I agreed.

About an hour later Sam phoned. 'A fine specimen you found there, Angus. He was in grand condition. That's him all done for you; rump, fillet, legs and chops.'

I went to collect him; Sam had all his parts individually wrapped for me. I made him promise not to say anything to Laura as she would be horrified.

'Sure, Angus, your secret's safe with me, I'm just like a doctor I'll sign the '**butchercratic oath**.' He belly laughed. 'Enjoy Mr Fox.'

We served Mr Fox at several dinner parties. Laura never knew and Sam kept the **'butchercratic' oath.**

I'm glad Mr Fox didn't die in vain. No more roadkill I vowed.

Then I saw it while driving. A dead body?

## THE IRISH BOAT

We walked to the Broomielaw, living in Anderston it was just minutes away, easy to walk to. I was around age 4 or 5, mesmerised by the big ship. It was in fact the cattle boat ferrying cattle to and from Ireland. Known by Glasgow locals as the Derry Boat or the Irish Boat.

I was so excited to board the ship. There was always a great big queue, people with tattered old luggage; ours included. We travelled steerage, down in the bowels of the ship with the cattle. That was the way poor people travelled. To me we were rich, I didn't know anyone who travelled to a different country on a big ship. I was impatient and couldn't wait to board. I would ask, 'mammy why can't we go on now?' 'Hau'd yer wheesht' she would say, 'It won't be long.'

We would lug our suitcases downstairs then grab a seat against the wall. The funnel would hoot, and we'd be sailing down the Clyde out into the Irish Sea. Up on deck we would wave to all the dockers who worked in the shipyards. 'Shipyards are sadly all gone now.'

My wee Irish Granny Ellen Jane would not dare go on deck. She sat upright all night clutching her Rosary Beads, moving her lips in prayer.

The Irish Sea could be wild, people would be sick through the night. I can imagine it must have been stinking. Sweaty bodies and spew not to mention the cattle next door, but to me it was magical, just like all my childhood memories.

In the morning everyone was up on deck with their luggage waiting to disembark. We sailed up the River Foyle into Derry City with its two Cathedral spires. St Columba's Church of Ireland, and St Eugine's the Catholic Church. Very similar in architecture.

We had breakfast with my mother's cousin George Hamill and his wife May who lived in Waterloo Street. Their back yard was surrounded by Derry's Walls.

Then we'd move on to Strabane to visit Mary Jane, another of my mother's cousins. I can't remember how we travelled. Bus, train or maybe a jauntin car? It would be lovely if some were still alive to ask; but sadly not. Mary Ann had a rocking chair. I loved it. We would stay overnight with Mary Ann.

The next day was my favourite part of the journey. Again, I don't know how we got there? We travelled to Plumbridge in Co Tyrone known as the Plum. The Plum is a sleepy little village at the foot of the Sperrin Mountains. With the Glenelly River gurgling through its centre.

We again lived with cousins. Cassie Black (McCullagh) was My Granny Ellen Jane's cousin. They were nearly all McCullagh's in the Plum. Cassie's father was a blacksmith, hence the name Cassie Black.

Cassie lived in a lovely, whitewashed cottage with a huge open fire that dominated the room. There were chickens, cats, kittens, and a big sheepdog. I chased them all wanting to pick them up apart from the dog. The poor things ran for their lives when they saw me. Every night we'd sit by the fire, there was always someone playing a fiddle. All the adults would sing the old Irish come all ye's. Most old Irish songs started with come all ye.

Stories would be told of fairies and banshees. I was mesmerised, I always wanted to meet a fairy but not a banshee. 'Can I meet a fairy, Cassie?' Sure, ye can, now go to bed and you'll meet a fairy in the morning.' I could hardly sleep in anticipation of meeting a real fairy. Sure, enough the next morning under the window there were two wee fairies sitting on the bench. Mrs. Salt and Mr. Pepper.

 Did they think I was daft? I thought I would have seen two wee dancing fairies.

Then there was the well! Cassie's daughter Kathleen would take me up to the well every day to collect fresh water, they had no running water in the cottage.

Kathleen would drop the bucket that was attached to the well, collect the fresh water then transfer it into the bucket she had brought with her. I always asked if I could do it, but she wouldn't allow me to in case I fell in.

I chased the poor animals, patted the dog and fed a lamb. I loved every minute of it.

Alas it was time to go home on the Derry Boat back to the fog and dingy old Glasgow. For me the Plum was like living in paradise. My poor wee Granny Ellen Jane would always ask when back in Anderston. 'When am I going home?' meaning the Plum. Sadly, she never did. She died in Glasgow.

I have since returned to the Plum. Nothing much has changed. Cassie Black's house is now converted into a nice modern bungalow; there's a Spar shop. The original pub is still there. 'The Glenelly Bar.' The graveyard would you guess? Is full of McCullaghs. When we did go back to the Plum, it wasn't on the Derry boat. It was Easy Jet. But all the memories are still with me.

## THE BEAUTY I SEE

Driving down from Inverness

Through lochs and mountains to impress

We were sad to say adieu

Carried on through the A82.

On to Ben Nevis

Britain's Highest Mountain

Snow Capped beautiful.

Astounding

Then to my favourite place

The Valley of Glencoe

Haunting mist reminding me

Of that slaughter long ago

Lochs rivers and mountains

All of the way

Thank you, Bonnie Scotland,

For a magical day

## GODS GIFT

He thought he was God's gift

Woman swarmed around him.

He staggered here he staggered there

Never out the gym.

Then one day he asked me out.

Was he blind and couldn't see

This Adonis of a man

Wanted little me.

He asked we go to dinner.

I just said OK.

He said you must provide the goods

If you want me to pay.

I stared at this hunk of a jerk

My next step took some guts.

Oh! 'Yes' I said here are the goods

And kicked him in the nuts.

## MAGS AND TAM

MAGS   Will you stop doing that Tam, It's embarrassing.

TAM   Shoosh Mags, they're talking about someone in the hotel.

MAGS   You're so nosey. What does it matter?

TAM   Wid ye shut up?

MAGS   It is so rude. These are people you don't even know and will never see again.

TAM   They're talkin' aboot a wee wuman is this hotel.

MAGS   Whit wee wuman, I've never seen a wee wuman?

TAM   Would you just shut up Mags. They're saying they cannae get tae sleep at night. A cannae hear the rest for you buttin' in awe the time.

MAGS    For goodness' sake Tam, if you don't stop listening in to other people's conversations I'm moving to another table.

TAM     Wait, wait. They've just said they're in room 202

MAGS    Room 202 that's next door to us. What are they saying?

TAM     Oh! Noo yer interested? He's saying to the other couple that they cannae get a wink o' sleep fur the wee wuman next door, farting and snoring.

MAGS    That must be the couple at the other side of them. Not us.

TAM     There is no one at the other side of them. They are at the end of the corridor.

MAGS    Well that must be you they're talking about.

It's certainly not me.

TAM  Haud oan, they're saying something else.

MAGS  I'm moving table.

TAM  They're saying that they know it's the wee wuman farting and snoring 'cause they hear her man telling her to shut it.

MAGS  I'm not listening to this anymore, I don't believe any of it.

*Mags gets up in a huff, storms out the door farting like a trouper.*

## AN UNFORTUNATE AFFAIR

Jan shouted, 'I'm away out. Alec.' What, again Jan; where are you off to now'? 'Just a bit of shopping, maybe meet Cathy for a coffee.'

Jan was out an awful lot lately. It wasn't like her. Three times last week and twice this week. What was she up to? Alec decided to find out.

Jan returned with no bags. 'I thought you had gone shopping?' 'Och, I just met Cathy and we had a wee bit lunch and a long chat. I'm away for a bath to relax.'

As soon as Alec heard Jan splash into the water, he was on the phone. 'Oh, hello Alec how are you?' 'I'm fine Cathy. Jan is in the bath, she asked me to phone you. Did she leave her scarf while you were having lunch?' Cathy paused, hesitated a bit too long. 'Eh! I didn't see Jan today Alec. Maybe it was Katy she met?'

Alec rang Katy. 'Hello Katy, I just wondered if Jan Left her scarf while you had lunch today?' 'Sorry Alec, I didn't have lunch with Jan today. It must have been Cathy.' Alec was confused. 'What was she up to?'

Next morning Jan got up early and had breakfast. She kissed Alec on the cheek and said, 'I'm off to get the shopping darling, see you soon.?'

'Ok love, see you later.' As soon as Jan got into her car Alec jumped into his. He followed her at a safe distance. She pulled up at a neat terraced house about a mile away; got out of the car and rang the bell.

A well dressed man in his 50's opened the door and kissed Jan on the cheek. I couldn't believe it. In all our married life I would never have thought that my wife would cheat on me.

We were both in our 50's, had good marriage, an empty nest. Independent children. I had taken early retirement and we had planned to take nice holidays together. What was she thinking? I was raging.

I never mentioned what I had witnessed when she returned with "the shopping." I continued to follow her, and the same thing happened each time.

I was determined to get revenge. How dare this man seduce my wife. I sat outside his house for a few days getting to know his routine. Each day around three he went out and walked to the local shops.

I now felt I was ready to put my plan into action. I sat watching. Then he came out prompt on three. He had to venture up a quiet lane to reach the shops. I made sure no one was around.

He went flying into the air and came down with a loud bang. I didn't hang around to see what happened. I was sure he was dead. Justice was served.

Jan went out the next day as usual. I thought. This will be your last visit my love. It wasn't long before she returned. Not with the shopping but with a little bundle of fur.

'What the hell is that?' I asked. 'This is McKay.' she said with a slightly sad look on her face. She took the most adorable little pup out of a blanket. 'Where did you get him?' I said, looking puzzled.

'Well! The most unfortunate thing happened. I had booked this puppy before he was born. After the bitch had her litter, I went to visit them. I was going to Mr McKay's home nearly every day to visit the pup. I had to bring him home sooner than expected. His poor owner was knocked down by a hit and run driver. His wife now has carers, she is in a wheelchair and housebound.' I bought this little fellow to make the house a home again since the children left.'

'Mr McKay didn't die. He has broken ribs and a fractured pelvis. He was lucky, even managed to get the end of the driver's license plate. The police are looking into it as we speak. Why darling! You've gone quite pale. Hold on there's someone at the door.'

## JUST WAN MAIR

Ellen      Where ur ye?

Jim      Doon the Bay.

Ellen      Whit time da ye want me tae pick ye up?

Jim      Haulf five

Ellen      Ye better be ready?

Jim      A will, don't want tae be doon here awe night.

Ellen      Ok! but I know whit yer like.

Ellen      It's haulf five, I'm comin' doon tae get ye.

Jim      Kin ye just give me 5 minutes; big Al his just goat me a drink

Ellen      You're a feckin' nightmare. Just make yer ain way up.

Jim      Yer no askin' me tae walk up that hill ur ye?

Ellen      Ok I'll come doon but ye better be ready mind, 'cause I'm no waitin' oan ye.

Jim         'Course I'll be waitin' oan ye darlin'.

Ellen       Don't you darlin' me, a know whit yer like.

Jim         I'll be ready.

Ellen       Am ootside and its bloody freezin', hurry up?

Jim         Dae ye want tae come in fur wan? A had tae get big Al a drink back.

Ellen       Ach ok, but jist wan mind.

Jim         Are you ready tae go?

Ellen       Naw

Jim         You're a feckin' nightmare.

*Needless to say, we both staggered up that feckin' hill*

Printed in Great Britain
by Amazon